ROYAL REBELLION
SISTERS OF ANDLUSAN DUET

ANDIE M. LONG

This book is a work of fiction. Names, characters, places and incidents are either the product of the author's imagination or are used fictitiously, and any resemblance to actual persons, living or dead, events or locales is entirely coincidental.

No part of this book may be reproduced or transmitted in any form or by any means, electronic or mechanical, including photocopying, recording or by any information storage and retrieval system without the written permission of the author, except for the use of brief quotations in a book review.

Copyright (c) 2018 by Andrea Long
All rights reserved.

Cover by Jay Aheer at Simply Defined Art.
Formatting by Tammy Clarke at The Graphics Shed

LAST RITES

CHAPTER ONE

Mercy

The excitement made me feel so alive. My heart beat faster in my chest, and adrenaline ran through my veins like a rabbit at the start of a hunt.

In the passenger seat of the car, my thighs stuck to the leather with sweat. The windows were open, and strong gusts of wind whipped my hair like a piece of plastic caught in a tree. The brown locks fell over my eyes and for a second or two I couldn't see, obscured by my collagen curtain. An unknown to me song, with a deep bass beat that thrummed through my chest, boomed from the car stereo. My grin was fierce, my eyes twinkling with the excitement of the rush, a life being lived to the max.

We sped down the country lanes, the undulation of

one dip making my stomach flip. A car on the opposite side of the road sounded its horn.

"Fuck off, you miserable old bastard." Billy yelled. No doubt the driver had forgotten what it ever felt like to be young. I could imagine his passing glare fixed in cantankerous judgement. I raised my hand to move the hair once again blocking my view and then time slowed down to thousandths of a second. Life in infinitesimal motion.

Billy turned to me and I was struck by the raw beauty of his face. The jut of his jaw and the angles of his cheekbones. His perfect silver-grey gaze as his eyes met mine, widening before me. His perfect white teeth as his mouth opened in a silent scream. His thigh tensed on the brake, pumping down on something no longer working. The barrier protecting the trees and the hills now stood out in my vision as it came ever closer...

Then there was silence, and I stood among the wildflowers and heather, my cornflower-blue gossamer gown billowing in the breeze.

White feathers fell from the sky like an angelic snowstorm, pooling around my feet as if I stood on a cloud.

Billy stood to my side as we gazed out from the hilltop.

"Am I dead?" he asked.

"If you are, then I'm dying too." I looked down at myself, watching as my body shimmered like a hologram.

Billy's mouth gaped. "What's happening? Are we ghosts?"

"Wait for me. Hold on. I can save you." The portal opened down below on the other side of the hill, out of Billy's sight. My way home and my way of saving him. So, I jumped, leaving him standing there.

Leaving him thinking God knows what.

Leaving him stuck in limbo.

I jolted awake, my breath coming in short pants. Thank Goddess, it was just a vivid dream, a nightmare. Slowly, I raised myself up on my feather pillows, noticing that my skin was clammy, my bedclothes and nightdress damp with perspiration. I rang the bell on my bedside table and my lady-in-waiting, Saira, came straight through the door.

"Morning, Your Highness."

"I wish you'd stop this nonsense and call me Mercy." I told her for the millionth time.

"You're second-in-line to the throne and I will always call you Your Highness. Well, to your face that is." Saira winked.

I shook my head laughing. "Could you draw me a

bath please? The night was hot, and I need to feel clean."

Saira walked around to the side of my bed where she drew back the assortment of blankets. Here at the Winter Court we always sought comfort in our bedcovers and I was no exception. My bedroom was painted a beautiful ice-blue colour, and warm blankets were covered by an exquisite tapestried cover of individual snowflakes which had took a seamstress a year to complete.

I was a Princess of the Winter Court. Our mother had passed away a month ago after succumbing to an infection, and now myself and my twin sister, Leatha, were the next generation of royalty. At a few minutes older than me, it was Leatha who would sit on the throne as Queen, and I would be named the Queen's consort, until such time as Leatha married.

Where I accepted my fate, Leatha did not. We were as different as identical twins could be. We were mirror images, but for the fact I had a small mole above my lip. Leatha hated being in the Winter Court. She wanted to travel, to see the other Kingdoms. She spent hours reading books about imagined lands such as life on the planets of Earth, Mars, etc. Leatha was given to fancy and could barely be raised out of her chambers before midday, lost in books and her dreamworlds.

I knew we had the responsibilities of our people in

our hands, and although our Court suffered no real hardships at present—despite the challenges of living in a permanent winter—we had a duty to ensure that each and every villager had an ear to listen to them should they require it.

Leatha's coronation was in three days' time. Yesterday she had been almost impossible to speak to and spend time with.

Leatha burst into my room where I sat at my desk tending to paperwork left by our mother's secretary—now our secretary. And so it would be that I would take care of such matters because my sister would pile them on a desk and make paper aeroplanes out of them imagining that each one was taking her on a journey outside of the Winter Court.

She threw herself upon my bed, laid out on her back, and sighed.

"My life is over before it's even begun, Sister. I shall be forced to marry for position, not pleasure, and to stay here in the Winter Court, my zest for life frozen like the landscape of this boring place. I may as well end myself."

I turned in my chair to look upon her.

"There is much adventure awaits you as Queen.

Look at all the balls we shall hold. How visitors from other Kingdom's shall come bearing gifts to honour and to beg favour of the Queen. How many pretty gowns shall fill your closets. All the women of the land, especially the younger girls, shall want to be you, Leatha."

Another sigh. "I suppose." She bolted upright and rolled onto her stomach, elbows bent and resting her chin on her hands. "I could get the seamstresses to make me dresses so utterly splendid that everyone will hold their breath to see me and gasp at their magnificence. Some may even faint with the wait."

"I'm sure a few will." I encouraged her. This was the only way to get my sister interested in her future position.

"And of course, you shall also have beautiful gowns, but none so beautiful as mine. Where mine will be festooned with jewels, yours shall complement the colour but be plainer."

I kept the smile on my face, though right now I wanted to become the ten-year-old me, where I would jump on the bed and pull her hair for being mean.

Leatha jumped off the bed with the same gusto as to which she'd first leapt upon it.

"I'm off back to my room to call the seamstresses to come take an order for more gowns. And to ensure my coronation gown is the most decadent thing anyone has ever seen."

It already weighed so much she could barely move in it, but I let her leave the room and take her wild ideas with her while I buried myself back in the paperwork.

Saira had prepared me a breakfast of oats and berries for after I had finished bathing. I had almost finished eating when a knock rattled my door like a cannon had fired at it.

"Your Highness. Your Highness." A woman's shrill voice could be heard from the other side. I got up from my seat but Saira had gotten there before me and opened the door to reveal Ramona, my sister's main lady-in-waiting.

Ramona stood trembling as she whimpered words it took time for me to decipher. "Princess Leatha. Something is wrong. Come quickly. I have phoned the royal physician."

I dashed from my room although I was dressed only in my undergarments: long-johns and a vest top.

My sister's room was on the other side of the top of a vast staircase. My chambers to the right, hers to the left.

As I burst into the room, what I saw took my breath away.

My sister was lying on the bed on her back looking

as if she were mid-nightmare. She tossed and turned though no sounds came from her mouth, but the worst thing was her body was turning translucent. It disappeared, then re-appeared fully. It kept changing between the three states.

"Dear Goddess, what is this?" I gasped. I had heard of magic, but I had never witnessed it before. This could not be anything else because people didn't just disappear before your eyes.

"Someone must have placed a hex on her, or something. Maybe an enemy who does not wish to see her take the throne?" Ramona queried. "But I don't know how as no one has visited her quarters. She was asleep in her room at ten pm last night."

"And you just found her like this? It is now ten am, that's twelve hours she could have been like this."

"Yes, your sister won't allow me to assist her before this time of the morning."

I knew this already, and I also knew I needed to keep outwardly calm, though inside me terror was giving me chest pains, and the sound of my heartbeat thrashed in my ears.

Our main physician, Lord Thomas Mandrake, knocked on the door and entered the room. I looked at him and watched as his face paled. He was a tall, thin man, with dark hair, who looked older than his actual age, as if life had bore down heavy on him. I was very fond of him. He had always been close to our family, and I considered him like I would an uncle. He had no wife or children of his own, preferring to spend his time caring for the sick and infirm.

"Oh no. Please no."

"What is it?" I yelled at him. "Tell me."

He looked at the ladies-in-waiting.

"Please excuse us." I asked them. "If you could wait outside the door, I will call you if you are needed. Please do not let your faces show that there is anything wrong with Princess Leatha. If anyone asks, she is troubled by a severe headache brought on by the pressure of her upcoming coronation."

Saira and Ramona both nodded and quietly left the room.

I looked back at Lord Thomas.

"I need to check your sister over and see if my initial assessment and my fears are confirmed." He told me. "Could you assist me?"

"Of course."

"When she appears in solid form, please grab her hand. It should keep her grounded for a little longer than usual."

I walked to my sister's bedside. Where my top blanket was festooned with snowflakes, she had chosen for hers to be covered in silver threaded sigils and white feathers. She had heard fanciful stories from our grandmother that we were descended from a family of witches and protected by angels. My grandmother had always been one for a tale, and whereas I had politely listened for the minimum time I could get away with before returning to studies that would benefit me in life; Leatha had sat for hours at her feet enchanted.

With her long dark hair, hung in waves around her pale-skinned face, Leatha looked like a sleeping angel.

As her shimmering form solidified, I grabbed her hand, noting the ice-cold touch of her fingers within my own.

"Well done." Lord Thomas checked her eyes, her pulse, and then he murmured an incantation under his breath. My sister's skin took on a purple hue, and I gasped and let go. She disappeared, returning and shimmering again after a minute. A minute in which I thought my heart would stop beating.

"It is as I feared." Lord Thomas turned to me, a grave expression on his face.

"Your sister has been abusing magic. She has been travelling the planes to visit places not of our kingdoms. She has become stuck. Something must have happened to her, an accident or tragedy where she visited, and now she is between worlds."

"So, we find someone who is an expert in magic and we get them to free her." I ran a jerky hand through my own dark hair.

Lord Thomas reached out and took my free hand, clutching it in his own.

"I am sorry, Princess Mercy. When someone is between worlds, they live in eternal torment lest we end that misery. I will need to perform the Last Rites ceremony to free your sister."

"What? Are you telling me she must die?"

He nodded. "I am sorry, there is no other way."

"There must be." I snapped. "Get me a magician to talk to."

"Magic is banned in this realm as you well know."

"I know that I am not going to allow my sister to die." I held his gaze.

Lord Thomas leaned in closer to my ear and whispered. "There is a peace spell I was taught earlier on in my career. I can cast it now, but it will only last a few days. Your sister will just look as if she is sleeping."

"Do it. Please." I urged. "Buy me some time."

He stood over her bed and I watched as he whispered the words that stopped her slipping in and out of the world.

"It is only temporary." He told me. "You have only days, maybe three or four."

"So I have until the coronation to try to find a way to get my sister back?" I looked around her room at the masses of books piled on tables. Maybe there would be something here to give me an idea as to where she had gone?

"Thank you, Lord Thomas. I will not forget I owe you a debt."

He chewed on his bottom lip, lost in thought for a moment. Then he fixed his gaze on me once more. "Should you find you have need to learn more about the magic arts, questions... please find me. I know someone who might be able to help. A friend's son. I should send him to you in the guise of an artist, sequestered to make a coronation gift for your sister."

"We are very honoured indeed to have such a faithful physician. I thank you, Lord Thomas, and give you my blessings for a safe journey home."

With a bow and a doff of his hat, he bid me farewell. I sent the two ladies on their way with tasks to do, having reassured them all would be well and then I turned back to my sister's room.

It was time to start looking for clues.

CHAPTER TWO

Aaron

Our mother put cold water in her mug of red-hot black coffee and gulped it down at breakneck speed before staring at the kitchen table, her eyes widening.

"William Buckley. Out of bed before midday? Are my eyes deceiving me?"

My brother Billy sat back in his seat, his hands behind his head as if he had all the time in the world. Which he did because he was a student and it was the final days of the summer holidays. At a year older, I was off to my job working as a manager in a store that sold sports clothing and equipment. Academia hadn't been my thing whereas Billy didn't even need to revise.

It all just came naturally to him. I'd spent years feeling like a dumb older brother, but my gift was my gab. I could sell 'snow to Eskimos' as they say and I was climbing the corporate ladder fast, already deputy manager after only a year. So our mother was off to her job as a nurse at the local hospital, and I would be following shortly behind her. What my brother was up to was anybody's guess because he certainly did not get up at this time—ever. My mother's eyes met mine over the top of her mug, and she shook her head before placing it on the worktop.

"Right, boys, I gotta dash. Have a great day at work, Aaron. Billy, wash the dishes and for God's sake clean your room. I saw the open door and all I can see is laundry piled everywhere. Put it in the wash basket, or even better, try putting a load in. Only your own though, I don't want my clothes ruined."

"Thanks for the vote of confidence, Mum." Billy lifted up his thumb.

I waited until the door banged shut behind her before I stared my brother down.

"What are you doing today?"

"Nothing. I just couldn't sleep, that's all, so figured I may as well get up."

"I call bullshit, Bro. Is it Thea again?"

Thea Queen had moved to Hallbridge a few weeks

ago. She was a girl of mystery. All long dark hair, brown eyes, and secrets. From what I'd seen of her when she'd come around to the house, she was a closed book, giving little away about why she was here. She was beautiful, sexy, and yet I couldn't warm to her. I should have envied my brother having her attention, yet something about her left me cold. She seemed to have a hold over Billy, and I worried about how he'd be with his studies if she continued to hang around. Yes, he was naturally clever, but he still needed to study, and his attention needed to be focused on his exam year so he could go to university to study his passion—history. He hated it when I called him a nerd, but the truth was, I envied his passion. My own prospects were to manage a store, but there was no enthusiasm behind it. It was a means to an end. A bit like the relationship I'd just finished with Louisa Scott. She'd been sex, nothing more. When she wanted more, I'd ended it. No commitments, because at any point, given an opportunity for better things, I was out of this town. Hallbridge was a small, boring, very ordinary town, and I would hate to think I'd die in the same place I'd been born without ever having seen anything else.

It was an identical copy of most towns in England. The same shops in the centre as anywhere else. The same pockets of housing for the rough and ready where you were overlooked on every side by neighbours; versus the better sides where the houses were set back from wide, tree-lined streets, with basically their own parks as gardens. Thea lived in one of the better houses on the other side of Hallbridge. Billy had never explained why she hung around here in Misley. Where we lived was in 'average land', our home a semi-detached that Mum had kept after the divorce from our father. We'd never heard from him again. Mum had never married again. She refused to talk about him, and we found mention of him upset her so much that we stopped asking.

"It's the last few days of the holidays. I've told Thea that I'll not be able to see her so much, so she's making me hang with her all day today."

"Doing what? Oh my god, don't answer that." I said quickly.

"We've a whole schedule planned, and yep hopefully that's on it."

"You might want to make a start on that room then." I told him.

"Oh shit, yeah."

I don't think I've ever seen my brother move so fast. After I'd spent a good couple of minutes laughing, I stood at the sink and washed the dishes that I knew he'd never get around to, and then I set off to work.

Why had I slept with Louisa? Louisa who worked in the coffee shop a few doors down. Louisa who was standing in front of me at this very moment with a latte in a cardboard cup in her hand.

"Here, Aaron. It's hot… just as you like it. You got a break soon? I could get our staff room for a short while. We're short-staffed today and it's quiet."

"Sorry, Louisa. I'm enjoying a different brand of coffee from now on." I told her, making it plain that I was no longer interested. "Yours has been lovely, but I'm all for trying something new. Now, if you're short-staffed maybe you should get back to help your colleagues out. That's what they're paying you for, right? Not to bring the goods out and give 'em away free."

She threw the coffee at me. Thank Christ I took it so milky, or I'd have been visiting the Accident & Emergency department. As it was, my sports attire dripped with foam, and puddles of the brown liquid pooled at my feet.

"By the way, I don't fuck in staff rooms. I only fuck in beds, on sofas, and against walls. Not in goddamn communal areas in shithouse coffee shops."

"I fucking hate you, Aaron Buckley."

"Then my job here is done."

I watched as Louisa turned on her heel and stomped off out of the store. Then I picked up the discarded carton from the floor and headed to our own staff room to clear up the second drinks detritus of the day. Then I got changed.

"She's barred." Melanie, the store manager told me having approached once I was back on the shop floor. "You agree to no more fucking of any of the staff in this shopping centre, and I'll take the coffee soiled laundry home." Mel was ten years older than me and had three kids. She was like a bossy big sister.

"Deal. I'm off women for a while. Too much drama." I said.

She laughed. "You keep pretty and single, darling, and get all those teenage girls coming in after school buying whatever they can afford, or scrounge off their parents, in the hope you'll notice their desperate faces. I like to watch so I know what to expect when my three grow up, seeing as they're as handsome as their mother is pretty." She winked and went back to serving.

It was a long day. I worked from ten am to eight pm, five days a week, on a rota between Mondays and Saturdays. It took twenty minutes to drive home and then I needed to fix myself something to eat, or warm up anything my mum may have made for us that had escaped Billy's greedy mouth. So it was always around nine-thirty before my arse eventually parked itself on the sofa.

Home that night, I switched the TV on to find anything to stare at while I chilled out, finally settling on an episode of Wheeler Dealers. Mum wasn't home. I figured she'd gone out with her best friend. Her car wasn't there.

The next thing I knew I was startled from sleep by my mother pushing at me frantically. "Aaron! Is your phone not on? I've been trying to call you."

We didn't have a house phone. We'd felt there was no need in this day and age. Except I was useless at charging my mobile. I found my phone a nuisance rather than a benefit. "Damn, I must have let it run out of juice again." I rubbed my eyes, though I was coming around quickly due to the wide-eyed, frantic expression on my mother's face.

"I'd got a headache when I got home, so I went straight to bed. Billy and Thea were here when I got in. I asked if they'd keep the noise down, and so they said they'd go out. When I woke an hour ago my car was gone, Aaron. I can't get hold of him. Why would he be so stupid to take my car out? He doesn't have a full licence. His test isn't until next week. I don't know if it's been stolen or he's taken it because I can't get hold of him to ask, and I can't go looking properly because I have no frikking car. I've been walking around the estate but no one's seen him." She scrubbed a hand through her hair. "Can you take me out in your car, Aaron, and do you know where he might have gone? It's so out of character for him."

"Sure, Mum. I'll put my phone on charge in the car too. He might have messaged me." I placed my hand on her shoulder and squeezed. "We'll sort it. He'll be showing off to Thea, that's all. You know what a swot he is. He could probably teach the driving examiner. He's just thinking with his cock, not his brain, I reckon."

A knock came on the door.

"That'll be him now." I reassured her. Billy often knocked the door even though he had keys. He was such a lazy arse.

But it wasn't Billy. It was the police. Two policemen who stood on the doorstep and asked if they could come in. Time slowed down to thousandths of a second. Life in freeze-frame.

I took my trembling mother's arm as we took seats on our sofa and listened to one of the policemen as he told us there had been an accident.

"We were notified of a collision on the Devil's Curve. A Vauxhall Astra." He described the car and read off the registration number and my mother crumpled in my arms. "I'm sorry. Your son was pronounced dead at the scene."

"No, no, no, no, no." My mother wailed.

"What about Thea?" I asked.

"Thea?" The policeman queried.

"Yes, his girlfriend. Was she not with him?"

My mum looked up. "He's been dating?"

Shock was obviously hitting her hard.

"Yes, Mum. Thea. You were talking about her earlier. You said they were in the house when you got home, remember? Then they went out."

My mum sat up and shook her head. "Oh darling." She turned to the policeman. "It must be the shock."

I could feel my temper rising.

"There was no one else at the scene of the accident. Only the young man we believe to be your son. It would appear by the tyre marks left, he had been in some kind of race or chase. Unfortunately, as you know that road has no cameras on it and is very dark with the tree canopy overhead. The car hit the corner barrier on the last turning before the main road. We will need you to come identify your son, Mrs Buckley. I am so sorry for your loss."

"She's got to be behind this... Thea. He would never have taken my mother's car before he met her."

"I'd better phone a doctor." My mother said, now wiping her eyes and trying to comfort me. But I didn't need it. Why was she unable to remember Thea?

Then I remembered. Billy had a photo of them

both as his screensaver. "Just a minute." I jumped up and ran to his room for his laptop. I paced while it fired up and then at last the picture came on screen. A picture of Billy and I, where he was wearing a tee saying 'I'm with this idiot' that pointed at me. A massive satisfied grin on his face while I'd genuinely thought he wanted a pic with his big brother.

I quickly clicked through his photos.

There wasn't a single picture of Thea.

Maybe I was going mad after all.

The evening was a nightmare as I went with my mum to identify Billy's body. My mind felt fractured. If I could make up a whole person and think she was real, then was my brother even dead? A doctor came to see us and prescribed something to help my mum sleep. I rejected any offer of medication. I needed to feel in control, to get my brain to sort itself out. But my body wanted to shut off. The shock was making my eyes close, anything to block out the fact that my beautiful younger brother was no longer living on this earth. My mind refused to accept this as reality.

Eventually, back home and in my bed in the early hours of the next morning, my eyes closed and trauma took me under into a tumult of disordered dreams.

. . .

The beeping of my alarm woke me up. Shit. I'd need to phone work and tell them I wouldn't be in for some time. God, how was my mum doing? I dashed from my room, saw her bedroom door was open, and then I took the stairs two at a time.

She was in the kitchen, making a coffee and singing along to the radio, dressed for work, like nothing had happened.

"Mum. What are you doing?"

She turned to me and laughed. "Well, I call it singing, but I know I sound like a strangled cat. As long as I'm enjoying myself though, yeah?"

She handed me a drink. "I suppose your brother won't get up any time before lunch." She said.

"Mum." I clutched her arm carefully. "Do you not remember yesterday? The crash?"

She looked at me strangely and then lifted her car keys off the hook. My mouth gaped open. How could the car keys be there? Mum only had one set, and they were in the car when it crashed.

"What crash?" My mum asked, a crease forming between her brows.

"Erm, nothing. I've been dreaming nonsense again."

"You always did have a vivid imagination."

I walked through to the living room and looked out of the front window. My mother's Vauxhall was parked outside absolutely fine.

It had all been a goddamn dream. A vivid freaking nightmare.

I collapsed onto the sofa and couldn't help the tears that came down my face.

My mum's voice came from the hallway. "I'm off, love. See you later. Tell your brother he's not spending the whole of the holiday like this." The door banged shut.

Once again time slowed down to thousandths of a second as my gaze turned to the cube calendar my mother kept on the shelf.

21 Aug 2018.

Four days ago.

My heart thudded in my chest. I was going insane. I needed a psychiatrist. The crash. Thea. It couldn't have all been a dream. No one dreams that vividly.

My mother's car set off down the drive and I rose to my feet watching through the window as her car—very real in front of my gaze—disappeared from view. I needed to check on Billy. Make sure he was in his room. Then I was taking the day off sick because something was very wrong with my mind.

And then she turned the corner. Turned and walked right up the road on the opposite side and as she reached directly opposite she stared right at our house, right through the window, and her brown eyes met mine. Thea.

But something else was off. Because this girl's gaze was warm.

CHAPTER THREE

Mercy

The first thing I needed to do really was to get dressed. But I didn't want to leave the room, so instead I walked over to Leatha's large closet.

Goddess, everything was so fancy!

Eventually I found a plain grey dress she'd pushed right to the back and put it over the top of my undergarments. That done I stood and surveyed the mess everywhere.

Where to start?

Deciding her bureau was the best bet, I strode over to it with purpose.

It looked like someone had picked up books and dropped them upon the bureau from a great height. They were on the top and in piles on the floor. I cleared the whole of the top of the bureau off and set about picking up one at a time, opening each book to make sure nothing was tucked inside. I perused the titles.

Destiny and Angels.
A guide to Magick.
Dreamwalking.
Spellcasting.

I hung my head in shame. I never came to my sister's room; she always found me, and I'd never considered the fact that might be because she didn't want anyone knowing what she was up to, including me. I carried on working my way through the books, piling them into some kind of order of theme until the floor around the bureau was clear. I knew I would need to read some of these books to see what Leatha might have done, but how would I know which one? Ink marks on the top of her desk suggested she wrote. Perhaps she had a notebook or diary around? Her bureau had three drawers, two of a decent size and one narrower one with a lock. There was nothing of note in the larger drawers, and of course, the narrower one was locked, with no sign of a key in sight.

Next I went to Leatha's dressing table, wading through ridiculous amounts of gaudy baubles hoping

I'd find a key there. I slammed my back against her dressing room chair with frustration.

If I had a secret key where would I put it?

Then it came to me.

Despite all her vast amounts of jewellery, Leatha always wore a locket around her neck that our mother had given her. Of course, the locket was decorated in rubies; she wasn't letting her standards drop. But maybe what I had considered an acknowledgement to our mother was in fact a close hiding place for a key.

I walked over to Leatha. Despite the fact she was unconscious I still spoke to her, hoping she could hear me.

"Leatha. I'm going to look at the locket on your neck, okay? I need to know if you keep the key to your desk drawer there. I really hope so because I need to know how to save you, Sis, and time is passing by quickly. When I get you back I'm going to make you pinky promise to behave, and you know such things are binding with us, remember?"

I lifted her hair away from her neck, reached for the locket and opened it. Sure enough, inside was a small key.

"Oh, thank you, Goddess."

I closed Leatha's locket and tenderly placed her hair back as it had fallen previously, then I made my way back to the bureau, slipped the key in the lock and opened the drawer. Inside I found a slim dark brown journal. Had anyone opened the drawer randomly, they would never have thought it anything to bother with, but as I lifted it I felt a buzz come from the journal through my fingers, like some kind of faint electrical charge. It took me by surprise and I almost dropped it. Opening the book, I found pages of notes and spells. There were no diary entries of what she may have been thinking or doing. It was just a collection of information. I'd heard of these before, from our grandmother. Leatha had made a grimoire.

I turned the pages, looking at spells about protecting yourself from malevolent spirits, calling upon the elements, and then eventually I found what I'd been looking for. The first clue of what Leatha had done. My eyes re-read the title.

A spell for a safe journey between realms

Was that was Leatha had done? Performed witchcraft? I read on.

Should you need to travel from the Winter Court elsewhere and vice versa you must ensure that you do this spell before travel. While it may appear you are travelling for only a split-second, while you are in the astral plane should you be unprotected, you would be at risk from malevolent spirits and becoming trapped.

Equipment:

Altar
  Sage
  Saltwater
  Amethyst stone
  Piece of paper
  Small Pouch

Ritual:

Ensure you are freshly bathed or showered.

Use your—or make—an altar and ensure your space is clean and fresh. Sprinkle saltwater around the room to further cleanse the area.

. . .

Draw a pentagram on the paper or something that symbolises your request. Place the amethyst stone on top.

Burn some sage leaves and blow the smoke over your stone and paper, also ensuring the smoke goes into all corners around your altar.

Kneeling at your altar, give thanks for all your blessings and request that your journey between realms be protected by the angels.

Raise your hands and say the following:

My guides hear my words and keep me from harm.
    Your protection within me, and my amethyst charm.
    May I pass through the planes
    Clear from all strife
    And bring blessings with me through my spirit life

Imagine a warm golden light entering your body from the top of your head, filling you with its bright glow, turning brilliant white as it blesses you inside and out with its protection.

Fold your paper and place that and the amethyst stone in the pouch and keep this on you while you travel.

Clear your altar.

You may now proceed onto your journey. Imagine your destination and say the following:

Send me in flight
    Oh, dearest friends
    And accompany me
    To my destination's end
    With my feet on the earth, the heat of fire
    Please assist me on travel and ensure I don't tire
    With the breath of air, the cleanse of water,
    I ask that you protect your daughter.

On arrival at your new destination close your eyes and give thanks for your safe journey.

I dropped the book onto the desk in shock. Goddess, was this what my sister had been doing? Travelling between planes? Where had she travelled to though, and what had happened to her, for her to have become trapped? My mind flashed an image of a car crashing into a barrier and then everything went black.

I came to, finding myself laid upon the thick carpet of my sister's bedroom, and everything that had happened that morning rushed back at me. Could it be that my nightmare was not one from my imagination at all, but somehow, I had received a vision of what had befallen my sister? Had she actually been travelling to Earth?

Of course she had. I shook my head as I pictured the thrill on the face I had seen in my dreams, the one I had thought was my own. If I could picture it again clearly, I would bet I would see no mole above my lip. It was not me in my dream, but my sister, and a mystery boy. But the car had crashed.

What was it she'd said to him?

"Wait for me. Hold on. I can save you."

And then she'd jumped into a portal. That was

where my sister was. Trapped and trying to get back here to Andlusan.

So now it was left to me to save her.

I knew nothing of magic. So the first thing I had to do was to devour the pages of some of these books, and keep her grimoire close.

I called Saira and asked her to bring me refreshments and something I could graze on throughout the day. I refused to answer the questions in her gaze, pretending I'd not noticed her anxiety. I had the food and drink placed on Leatha's dining table and made sure that the books she'd left out—unaware she would not return to clear them away—were now hidden at the back of her closet, to be taken out one at a time as I read them.

After a drink and a snack, I sat on my sister's couch and began to read.

~

I was still there at first light of the next morning, having napped when my eyes had tired from all the words floating in front of them. I had a basic understanding now of the stories of magic Leatha had been reading, but how I got from reading about it to rescuing my sister from being trapped, was a step I couldn't see how to take. My sister had been looking at these books for a long time; I'd had barely hours. What if I made a mistake and ended up trapped too? What did I need to do next? Could I say a spell and free her, or did I have to actually physically rescue her?

There was only one action I could think of taking. I needed to contact Lord Thomas and ask him to send his friend's son. But I couldn't do that until later in the morning. So I packed everything away and returned to my own chambers where I fell into an exhausted sleep.

There were no dreams or nightmares this time.

CHAPTER FOUR

Mercy

A day had already passed since we had found my sister in her tormented state. Time was running out and quickly. I had sent message to Lord Thomas and buried myself in Court paperwork until I heard news of his friend's son.

It was three in the afternoon when Saira came to tell me that I had a visitor in our receiving room. An Isaac Stafford was waiting for me there.

She fussed about me ensuring I was fit to be seen and I made my way to the room downstairs.

Our receiving room was all white walls and black furniture. I walked in to find a man who looked in his early twenties stood by the bookcase perusing the titles.

He turned as I walked in, removed his hat, and bowed to me.

"Your Highness."

"Sir." I nodded. "Thank you for coming to see me to discuss the *artwork* I wish to commission you to undertake."

A vivid green gaze met mine. "Ah yes, the very important task."

We stood while Saira took drinks orders and left.

The man held out a white-gloved hand. "I'm Isaac Stafford. Please call me Isaac. I find Sir more befitting of a man of some years, not my bare twenty-one."

"Only if you call me Mercy."

He raised an eyebrow.

"Well, when we're out of earshot anyway."

That earned me a smirk, just before Saira walked back in with a tea tray.

"Thank you, Saira. That will be all for now. Mr Stafford and I have much scheming to do."

Saira excused herself but I knew that my lady-in-waiting was no fool and wondered what she had surmised was happening with my sister, who I'd said I would tend to myself, only allowing Ramona in occasionally while passing Leatha off as being asleep due to tinctures given by Lord Thomas.

"Please take a seat and make yourself comfortable." I pointed to the sofa, while I took a seat on a chair opposite. "Isaac, I can't thank you enough for coming all this way. I am desperate to help my sister. Did Lord Thomas explain what has occurred?"

Isaac removed his hat and gloves and sat down in his fitted dark grey suit. Then he opened the buttons of his jacket. "That's better. I always feel like I can't breathe in all this finery."

I allowed myself a closer look at him. He had strawberry-blonde hair, eyebrows, and lashes. A creamy complexion was scattered with freckles and then there were those green eyes. He was a handsome man of a medium build. I'm sure Leatha would have been flirting with him had she been in my shoes.

He cleared his throat, and I realised that I had been in a dreamworld staring. "Lord Thomas did tell me what has been happening. That he believes your sister is caught between planes. Has anything else happened since Lord Thomas left?"

I told him of what I had found in her room, of her grimoire, and all the books of magic and witchcraft. Then I told him of my nightmare.

He listened intently and then took a deep exhale.

"I can help you, Mercy." He said. "However, there is something that you need to know first."

"Of course. Whatever it is, tell me. Is it a fee? I am of course expecting to pay for your services."

"No." He shook his head vehemently. "It is nothing like that." He licked at his top lip.

"I am from a family of sorcerers, Mercy. We live on the other side of the Winter Court, off-grid. Since your mother's rule, any signs of witchcraft were forbidden, and we have spent the last years in hiding. Before that we were able to use the land as we saw fit. You are from a family of witches, Mercy. From all the way down your bloodline. Your father was a warlock."

"Don't be ridiculous. My father was the Queen's consort, and a war hero killed in action when Leatha and I were two years old."

Isaac looked at me, his head tilted slightly and pity in his gaze.

"No. No, he wasn't."

I thought of my paternal grandmother sitting with Leatha telling her stories while my mother looked at her in disdain, asking her not to fill her daughter's head with such lies and fancy. I would never be able to ask my mother the truth, her secrets taken to the grave.

"Why would my mother lie to us and forbid the use of magic?"

"She lost her husband to it. She would not have risked her daughters too. That is what I was told anyway."

"So are you a sorcerer?"

He smiled. "I am. Yet you don't appear scared by

that fact. Why is that? I thought you'd be nervous I'd turn you into a toad."

I rolled my eyes at him. "I'm one for facts, not fairy tales, Isaac, and the fact is that I saw my sister appearing and disappearing with my own eyes. I have found her spell books with my own eyes, and I have dreamed of her crash in my own mind. Therefore, I have invited you here so I may learn more and be guided on how to rescue my sister. If you show me real magic and craft, then what else can I do but believe it?"

"You were not what I was expecting, Princess Mercy of the Winter Court."

I held his gaze with my own, hoping to communicate that I would take no nonsense. "I am myself. I can be no other."

He chewed on his bottom lip.

"You may have no choice."

"What do you mean?" I could feel the crease I knew appeared between my brows when I was vexed or puzzled.

"I will explain in due course, but before that we have a problem."

"There isn't time for problems, only solutions." My voice carried an edge of irritation.

"I'm glad you feel that way. You see you're going to have to trust me, Mercy. Trust a stranger and a sorcerer, no less. Because you only have a couple of days to get your sister back before the Last Rites are performed and you lose her forever. So the question is, will you do as I ask? Will you trust the stranger and sorcerer before you?"

I sighed. "What would you have me do?"

"I want to perform a spell. I believe that you are bound from using your craft. Your sister was able to use magic though. How could that be?"

"She believed my grandmother, who was forever feeding her stories of magic, which we thought were make-believe. Judging by the sheer amount of books on magic and witchcraft in her room, I should imagine she learned how to remove her bindings."

"I'm guessing your sister is not as fact-seeking as you?"

"No. My sister is thrill-seeking, and that is why we are in this mess. She will not have cared of the risks, just been overwhelmed by the possibilities."

"Are you not the slightest bit intrigued about what is beyond this kingdom?" His gaze fixed on mine.

I spoke honestly. "My mother brought us up to know our duty. That Leatha would be Queen and I would be her consort until she took a husband. It was never prudent to think of anything but the Winter Court. Such thinking would only be a distraction."

"Well, prepare to be distracted."
"What do you mean?"

"Your only way to save your sister is to go where she has travelled and live as her. You have to change whatever she did that messed with how life on Earth should have proceeded. You said the man in the car died. My guess is that Leatha caused this somehow, and that he was supposed to live. You have to go back, live in Leatha's body, and repair what she's done."

I shot up from the sofa.

"That is preposterous. I cannot travel to Earth. Plus, I am no sorceress. I am just a Princess who is good at paperwork. How would I know how to be on Earth anyway? I saw the clothes they wore in my dreams. They were nothing like what I'm used to wearing here. Plus, I can't learn magic and witchcraft in a few hours. I'd get stuck there. Alone."

"We can prepare you for it all. And you wouldn't be alone because I'm coming with you."

I swear I froze in place for a good ten seconds.

"Pardon?"

"I shall take the role of your older brother when we travel, and I will be there to coach you and assist. At any sign of trouble, I will transport you back to the Winter Court."

"But how would I explain my disappearance here?"

"You wouldn't need to. Time is a different entity

here. For all the time you spend on Earth, here it will have taken place in a matter of seconds."

I rubbed at my brow. "This is very difficult to get my head around."

"That's why you need me. I will give you the rest of the day to think on it. Because there is to be no doubt. There is a risk to yourself by travelling through the planes and who knows what situations you will encounter on Earth."

"I have to save my sister."

"Even if that meant sacrificing yourself?"

I drew in a sharp intake of breath. "Might I have to make that decision?"

Isaac shrugged his shoulders. "That's just it. I can help you, but I can't know what you'll have to do. That's why I say take the afternoon to think about things."

"No." I paced the room. "My sister is the rightful Queen, and my sister needs to live. I would indeed sacrifice myself to save her life. The hours here are running down. What do we need to do first again?"

"First, we need to remove the bind and let you experience your powers, your destiny, your heritage. You need to tell your staff you have commissioned me to paint you and then please get us a room, a studio, somewhere in this palace away from them. Then we can start."

"Do you need to collect anything from your home to help me?"

Isaac shook his head.

"Then I will have Saira prepare dinner and find someone to find us a room to use as a studio. We will retire there after dinner."

"Perfect. We can say I am doing some first sketches in preparation."

"Won't people need to see evidence of actual work?"

"And they will." He smiled. "You have yet to see evidence of any of my sorcery, but you will."

∾

Following dinner, I made sure no one was in the vicinity and I entered Leatha's chambers with Isaac. "I think it's best you see her first. I trust Lord Thomas' word, but if you have more skill with your craft, then maybe you may see something he has missed."

Isaac spent time checking her 'aura' before turning to me.

"I can confirm Lord Thomas was correct. So now let us go and begin your teachings."

We walked in almost silence to the far end of the East Wing of the palace. The palace was so vast we barely used a quarter of it, but all was kept in good order. I unlocked the door to a ballroom and switched on the lights. A fusty smell hung in the air, a sure sign of an unused room. Locking the door behind me, I walked over to the windows, drew back the drapes, and lifted the sashes to let fresh air in. And fresh it was. Nothing but crisp clear air in the Winter Court.

"This is perfect." Isaac picked up two chairs and brought them to the centre of the dance floor.

Nervously, I sat on one of the chairs. Thanks to my sister, here I was unchaperoned in a room with a man I had only known for a couple of hours. My mother would be turning in her grave.

But I had no choice but to trust him. And if Lord Thomas did, that was good enough for me. The man had tried to be a male presence in our lives given the absence of our father from us being three years old.

Isaac went into his rucksack and took out a packet of salt. He sprinkled it in a circle around our chairs. He then placed a black cloth between our chairs and put a black candle upon it. "This is to collect any negative energy." He lit the candle.

"I'm going to speak a few words and I want you to sit as still as you can. Let your body relax and just listen and focus on what I say. I have no idea what's going to happen, but I am here with you, okay? Mercy, I promise I will not let you come to any harm."

I nodded. I felt like I might bring back all of the

dinner I had just eaten. Taking a deep breath in, I tried to calm myself.

Isaac reached over and took my hand. His cool touch met mine, and I appreciated the warm gesture. He opened my palm and placed a white crystal inside, before closing my palm again, but he kept his hand on mine. I focused on the comfort of his hand being on mine, feeling that while we were connected I was safe.

"Are you ready?" He asked.

I nodded. I was never going to be any more prepared mentally than I was now.

"Okay. I want you to take a deep breath in and then back out. Follow my breath."

I did as he asked.

"Imagine that a white light is above you, it enters at the top of your skull and it fills you with its brilliant divine light. You might not see it at first." He said, just as I was about to say that exact thing. "But take a moment, relax, imagine it, and it will come."

And it did after a few moments.

"We thank you gods and goddesses for your strength, and for the power you share with us, your faithful disciples. I ask that you welcome Mercy back into your welcoming arms, for she has been hidden from sight. She is one of your daughters.

. . .

Earth calls air, calls fire, calls water.

Brings all to spirit, to surround this daughter.

Through winter, bring spring, summer, autumn too

Make her whole again

And bind her to you.

Make the blind girl see

What was hidden before

Give her the keys to the unlocked door.

A wind whipped, blowing the drapes high in the air, before it tore around the circle blowing at my hair. I opened my eyes and watched as the black candle winked out. Isaac stroked at my fingers as my eyes widened. "Stay with me. You're safe." He said, as the light blew out overhead, glass from the bulb tinkling to the floor. I smelled earth, and as I looked down, it appeared within the circle around our feet, vines appearing and trailing up my legs, disappearing beneath my robe.

"Isaac…"

"It's working. Keep calm."

That was easy for him to say. He didn't have plants tangling around his legs. They reached my knees and stopped.

Then a blast of water flew up from the middle of

the circle. It rose high above our heads and then fell down, leaving both of us soaked to the skin.

The wind dropped, the room went silent, the earth retreated, and we sat there, the only evidence of anything strange having happened our wet clothing, skin, and hair.

"There was no fire." I told him.

"Click your fingers." He said.

I clicked my thumb against my middle finger and a flame appeared at the end of it. I jumped and it disappeared.

"Do it again and imagine that the heat has dried us." Isaac encouraged. I tried it, but it didn't work.

"Close your eyes. Imagine the white light within you again, then open your eyes and imagine the spark."

This time the flame stayed on my fingers.

"Stare into it and imagine we are warm and dry. Picture it. Close your eyes again if you prefer."

I closed my eyes, and a minute passed.

"Mercy, look at me."

I stared at Isaac. Isaac who sat there perfectly dry. I felt at my own hair and face. Not a single drop of water remained.

He took my hand again. "I need to finish the spell."

He looked to the now unlit candle. "We thank you for your welcoming of Mercy into your great family. Blessed be."

Isaac smiled at me.

"I don't feel any different." I said. "I thought somehow I'd be changed."

"You're still Princess Mercy Elizabeth Northcote of Winter Court." Isaac smiled.

I smiled back.

"Thank you for your help. Now what?"

"Now I have today and tomorrow morning to teach you some basic witchcraft, protection spells and suchlike. And then we travel to Earth."

CHAPTER FIVE

Mercy

I had lived behind the veil of what magic could bring. Isaac was an extremely accomplished sorcerer, and he placed a spell on the palace staff that meant they were convinced my sister had gone to visit the Summer Court as part of her pre-coronation rituals. He called it a simple power of suggestion, but to my mind, that which could make others believe an untruth was anything but simple. How did I know that he was not saying such suggestions to me also? I had to trust him at his word, and at the fact that he had taught me more protection spells than I knew nursery rhymes. He had pretended to leave the Court, but we had worked late into the night and he had slept in a bed in the East Wing when I had to return to my own chamber. The next morning he 'arrived' to be greeted by Saira and once again, after breakfasting, we went through even more teachings. I was exhausted by the time lunch was upon us and felt I couldn't take in another word.

"Eat up. You'll need your strength for the afternoon." Isaac stated.

I watched Saira's eyebrow raise, and I blushed. Isaac realised what he had said.

"For sitting still for a long time takes great stamina." He added. "We shall need to accidentally bump into your sister so that I may capture her exact likeness. Twin or not, she will exude her own personality and I need to capture that."

"You will have to make do with photographs as she is on a sojourn to the Summer Court and will only be back just before her coronation."

"Ah, a pity." He replied, playing his artist role as well as any stage actor.

∽

Following lunch, I excused myself to take a rest, when actually I was taking a shower. I had left the East Wing room open so that Isaac could do the same. We met in the ballroom afterward and followed the ritual I had found in my sister's grimoire. And then it was time.

We knelt on the dance floor. The amethyst stone

and paper clutched within our held hands as we faced each other.

Isaac adjusted the words slightly but spoke the spell.

"Send us in flight
  Oh, dearest friends
  And accompany us
  To our destination's end
  With our feet on the earth, the heat of fire
  Please assist us on travel, and ensure we don't tire
  With the breath of air, the cleanse of water,
  We ask that you protect your daughter,
  and me, your son,
  Please grant us safe passage
  until our journey is done."

I heard an almighty crack and my body jerked in the strangest of sensations. My eyes had automatically closed while I accepted my unknown fate.

"Open your eyes, Mercy."

I opened them and looked at Isaac. And then I closed them and opened them again.

Isaac was kneeling in front of me still clutching my hand. He looked the same except he was wearing jeans and a dark-blue t-shirt. I wasn't sure how I knew what these things were called. I just did.

I couldn't help it. I giggled.

Isaac smiled. "What are you laughing at?"

"You look funny."

"You've not seen yourself yet."

I looked down to find myself also in jeans and sneakers, but I was wearing an orange t-shirt that was so short it showed off my abdomen. I let out a squeal. I hardly ever even showed off an ankle in Andlusan!

This caused Isaac to dissolve into a fit of laughter and he laid down giggling on the carpet. I took in my surroundings. I was on the floor of a living room. The room had beige walls, and dark wooden furniture. There was a television, a CD player.

"Isaac. How do I know what all this stuff is?" I asked him with a frown on my face.

"It would be rather obvious and boring if we had to teach you everything from scratch, wouldn't it? So magic prepares you."

"I'm going to explore." I told him, and standing up, I began walking around the house.

My legs felt strange inside the tight jeans and I kept trying to pull my top down. After a while, I reached what was obviously mine, or should I say Leatha's bedroom, and I opened drawers until I found a black top that covered me down to my bottom. I stared at myself in the mirror on the back on the door. *I'm still me inside,* I thought feeling a little calmer. I was just in Leatha's body dressed in weird shit. *Weird shit?* I didn't speak like that. It would take time to get used to these strange tweaks.

I heard footsteps behind me and Isaac walked up onto the landing where I went out to meet him. He opened a door and I could see inside was another bedroom. I followed and peered in.

"So this is my room. While we are here, I'm your older brother and there's just us, okay? Not that anyone else will question it anyway."

"So all I have to focus on is to find out what Leatha did and fix it?"

"You got it."

"Okay. Perhaps I should start to search her room then. See if I can find any clues here as to what she's been doing while she travelled the planes."

"I've put our paper and amethyst in my bedside table drawer, okay?" Isaac stood beside it. "Whatever happens, we travel back together or not at all, okay? I'm not losing you in the planes between realms."

"Got it." My stomach rumbled. The noise echoed around the room.

"Okay. Now seeing as time is not passing at home while we're here, and given we need to keep our strength up, I'm going to take you out for a burger and fries. Followed by ice cream. Yep, that's what we'll do."

"You've been here before, haven't you?"

"I might have visited Earth before." Isaac's eyes crinkled with mischief.

"But how will we pay for things? Andlusan money isn't going to spend here, is it? It'll just draw attention."

"Mercy, Mercy, Mercy. Will you just trust that the magic has this shit handled?" He reached into his pocket and took out a wallet, opened it and showed me the notes and coins inside. "Let's go." He nodded towards the stairs. "Are you ready for your first time in a car?"

∼

I was relieved to see it wasn't the one from my dreams, but still I trembled slightly as I sat back in my seat. Isaac reached over and fastened my seat belt for me.

"Ready?"

I took a deep inhale. "Yeah."

But I wasn't. As it set off, my eyes widened before I covered them up with the backs of my hands. We travelled by horses and carriage in Andlusan. This was blowing my mind and scaring me half to death. Especially when others on the road came so close.

Once again Isaac burst into guffaws. "Oh this is

going to be as much fun as it is a serious rescue mission. Your face."

I glared at him. "Is it my fault I'm in a strange place where I have to sit in fast moving metal that I have dreamed causes fatal accidents?"

His face fell serious at that comment. "Ah yes. Your dream. Sorry, Mercy."

"I shall only forgive you if this burger thing is worth it." I told him, lifting my chin haughtily.

∽

Boy, was it worth it!

We'd entered the fast-food restaurant. Its tables were all small and rectangular, a far cry from our exquisitely carved banqueting tables. I took a seat while Isaac went to order. He came back with what he explained was a cheeseburger. I bit into it and a flavour explosion hit my tongue.

Mustard and onion relish dripped from the corner of my chin as I demolished it. "That is so good. Can I have another one?"

I ate two more burgers and some fries. My stomach was groaning, but then I saw a child go to the ice cream machine and whirr out white goodness. He then decorated it with different types of candy and sauce.

"You want one?" Isaac asked, though he was already getting up to order.

I loved it. But it wasn't until the cold from the ice cream hit my mouth that I realised I'd not given any thought to the weather. I stopped mid-bite and ran outside, Isaac hot on my heels.

"What's up, Mercy?"

"It's warm." I told him. "The sun shines and it's warm."

"And you only just noticed?" He was once again amused by my behaviour.

I shoved him in the arm. "I've had a lot to take in."

"That you have. Now shall we get back inside before they tidy up the rest of your uneaten ice cream?"

∾

By the time we got back to the house, I was groaning and clutching at my stomach. "Dear Goddess. I am going to die."

"You are so dramatic. You aren't going to die, though you might suffer from some digestive issues. You've overeaten food you aren't used to. Go and lie down on your bed. We'll start our investigations tomorrow."

I didn't argue with him. I needed to sit up in bed still and straight and let this food settle.

On entering my room, I looked around for something to do. There was a magazine on the side and so I settled back on the bed. Soon I was so entranced in what I was reading that thoughts of my stomach left me entirely.

An hour or so later, feeling much better, I started looking around Leatha's room, heading straight for her desk drawer. But there was nothing of note to be found, just writing implements. I checked her wardrobe at the bottom, and checked underneath her bed. Still nothing. Then I started on her drawers. Underneath a pile of what were modern day undergarments, I eventually found a ruled book with a black cover. Opening it up I found it was Leatha's diary.

I took it back to the bed and began to read.

CHAPTER SIX

Mercy

Leatha's fancy script swept across the page. My heart panged for my sister in that moment as I took in her words, picturing her in my mind's eye.

It's August 2018 here on Earth! On Earth. Can you believe that? I had travelled to the different Courts so often now that I'd found it beyond boring. I knew I'd be able to travel to a different realm. Our gran had spoken the truth. I am a witch! Now that I am confident in my craft there will be no stopping me. Excitement, here I come.

And the best thing? Time stays still at home in Andlusan. So not one single person back home knows I am about to experience life here in this place they call Misley. Mercy would have stopped me without a doubt. I can hear her voice now in my head, 'You have your royal duties, Leatha. You must settle down and concentrate'.

I don't want to settle down.

I don't want to concentrate.

I don't want to be Queen!

So while ever I am here, and time does not pass at home...

Well, that's just perfection.

∽

I met some people my age in a coffee shop. Thinking I had nothing to lose, I just went and said hi as they looked the same age as me. They're in the Sixth Form of a school just around the corner from the coffee shop, but luckily, it's now the summer break. They think I live in a house at the other side of town even though I've never said anything. It's strange. They just accepted me straight away as a new person moved into the town.

There's a boy there. He's seventeen like me, and he is so good looking. His name is Billy. Billy Buckley. He sounds like he should be on stage.

∽

Billy saved me a seat today! I'm spending my time in the house watching films, television, and reading magazines. Anything this new crowd is talking about, I'm checking out. There was a mobile phone in the house when I got there, and I knew what it was! Magic is incredible. I'm also studying my craft more. I may make a love spell! Or perhaps I don't even need one if Billy is saving me a seat already.

∽

Only me and Billy showed up today because there was some trouble between the rest of the group. One of them, Aled, has apparently been selling drugs. I looked into what he was selling, researched it on the internet. It sounded like fun to me, to completely let yourself go in the moment. I said something similar to Billy, and he told me I was being stupid. He was angry with me. I'll be sure to not say anything like that to him again. Anyway, he must have felt bad for getting cross with me because he asked me if I fancied eating dinner at his house, rather than the cafe. We walked there. His mum was at work, and he fixed us bacon and egg. His brother was at home on a day off. Aaron is two years older than him. They look similar, but Aaron looks serious and no fun. Must be a sibling thing.

~

I met Aled in secret and he gave me some weed to try for free. I felt so mellow. He's going to get me some more. I told him I want to try everything. He grinned and said I was his kind of girl. Then he kissed me. It wasn't what I imagined my first kiss to be like. He smelled of stale cigarettes. Anyway, I'd been hoping it would be Billy who'd kiss me.

~

I tried more things, and I didn't like them. I also read about what some of them could do to you. So I told Aled that I didn't want anything else. He told me not to be such a spoilsport. He's ruining things. I'm trying to get closer to Billy, and Aled keeps coming and putting his arm around me. Tonight I told him to leave me alone, and he said no one got to tell him what to do. He scared me a little. I'm going to look at my spell books tonight and see if there's anything I can do. I'm not supposed to cast anything that can bring harm, but what if I need to be kept from harm myself?

~

Aled told me I was a prick tease today. I was so mad

that when I got home I called upon fire and asked for all his bad drugs to be destroyed. That wasn't wishing harm, right? It was protecting everyone else. The fire at his house didn't cause too much damage. Billy said Aled is keeping a low profile because his dealer is looking for him. He wants the money he's owed...

I asked Billy if he wanted to go to the cinema with me and while we were there, I reached over and held his hand. When we left he kissed me. It was like fireworks fizzed in my stomach. This was the kiss I had hoped for!

∼

The diary entries had all been from July and August 2018. I wondered what the date was today? I put my mobile phone on. Monday 27 August 2018.

Flicking through her diary I noted that the last entry had been that Friday evening, the 31st August. It read:

I heard Aled was talking shit about me. Who cares? I know I can take care of him now if I need to. Nothing came of my fire, no retribution. Me and Billy are spending the day together. I want to go for a drive tonight into the countryside and take a picnic. I'm going to give him my virginity though he doesn't know it. I'm sure he can guess though. We have done one hell of a lot of kissing. He hasn't passed his test yet, but he can drive. I watched him have a practice test. His mother has a car. I'm sure I can persuade him to take us out in it if it's worth his while...

Oh my goddess, Leatha. My sister had been living the life of a human girl and enjoying being ordinary. No royal duties, no sanctions. She'd been doing whatever she liked. But she'd messed with this Aled. Was what happened to her and Billy a tragic accident or connected with this guy? I needed to ask Isaac all about drugs tomorrow and show him the diary. For now, I needed to get to sleep because there was one thing in this diary I wanted to explore at first light. Under the entry about visiting, Leatha had written:

It's the strangest thing. Billy and the rest think I come from across town, but I only have to walk around the corner to get to their house. His brother drove me home with Billy the other night after I missed the last bus and it took twenty minutes. It makes absolutely no sense but who am I to question any of this? Tonight, I did a spell to show me Andlusan. I saw Mercy sitting at her desk pouring over the boring Court paperwork. I wish that just once she would let herself go and experience some life. She is in a prison of her own making and my heart bleeds for her. Why can we not rule the Court and also our own hearts? They'll make me marry for duty there. Why would I want to go home? I miss my sister, but I do not miss the Court.

My sister pitied me. At the bottom of the page was a sketch. Of this house and how she had walked to Billy's, plus his address. I set the alarm on my phone for five am, turned off my light and went to sleep.

～

The nightmare returned that night. This time I could feel the thrill inside me, the excitement for the speed we were going at. But this time I could hear thoughts.

Oh Aled, can't you see? I choose Billy, not you. He's my destiny. I'm sure of it. No one makes me feel as alive as he does.

And then it came again. Billy turned to me and his eyes met mine, widening before me. I saw his perfect white teeth as his mouth opened in a silent scream. His thigh tensed on the brake, pumping down on something no longer working. This time I heard his words.

"The brakes. They aren't working. Oh my god. Oh my god. I can't stop the car. I can't..."

I woke in my bed, convinced I could feel the breeze pulling at my gossamer gown. But I was still in the clothes I'd fallen asleep in. It was a while before I could close my eyes again.

~

As soon as my alarm beeped I quickly visited the bathroom to freshen up and then I left the house. I'd redrawn Leatha's map on my hand. Isaac had been softly snoring when I walked down the stairs and I hoped I'd be back before he woke. I wanted to see the house for myself and with any luck, a glimpse of the boy she was so fond of. The one I would need to get to know in order to save their lives.

I slowly turned the corner of the street and I looked at the house numbers. Deciding to stay on the opposite side so I wasn't spotted, I walked at what I felt was a natural speed. Then there it was. A semi-detached house with an empty driveway and oh shit, there was someone in the window.

Cold eyes met my own. I don't know how, but I knew this was the older brother, Aaron. Quickly I put my head down and turning around, I rushed back the way I'd come. Once I was out of sight around the corner, I ran as fast as I could go until I was back at my front door.

Closing the door behind me, I rested my back against it, my breath coming in large gasps. I felt eyes on me and I looked up to the top of the landing where I met Isaac's glare.

"This isn't going to work if you sneak out and don't tell me what's happening. We're a team, Mercy. You will have some of this to do on your own, but we prepare both mentally and using the craft."

"I'm sorry." I dropped my gaze to the floor. "I found her diary and I wanted to see him. The boy she was responsible for killing." I looked back up and Isaac's gaze was fixed on me with interest.

"I'm going to fix some coffee and breakfast. Can you get me the diary? I need to read it myself."

I nodded as he passed me on the stairs and then I headed to my room to pick up the diary.

∽

Isaac sat with a stony-faced expression. "So she'd experimented with drugs. Looks like this guy Aled wouldn't back off. Unfortunately, from today through to her saying she was going out in the car with Billy on Friday, we have nothing. No entries to tell us what happened between then and now. My guess is that she wrote something, but that we can't know it. That you have to experience every day as she did until we work out how to change things."

"You know so much about this." I sighed.

"You would have known more, had your heritage not been kept from you." He replied.

"Well, seeing as using it has resulted in my sister being trapped within planes of existence, I think maybe my mother was right to turn her back on it."

"That's such a blinkered view. It's the fact it was a mystery that made it so attractive to Leatha. Look at how you were with the burger and ice cream. How you gorged. That's what Leatha did, only with magic. Had it been part of her everyday world, she wouldn't have done this. It wouldn't have held the same excitement."

"Maybe." I hesitated. "Why are you helping me, Isaac?"

"Because our Queen is trapped and you can get her back. Because if I show you that your ancestry is nothing to be afraid of, then maybe my family can come out of hiding and live freely again, worshipping our gods and goddesses. Maybe our Queen will also worship them."

"Leatha could have decided she wants to run away with the circus folks by the time we're back home."

"Then why don't you take the crown?"

"Because I'm the youngest. Leatha has to be crowned. She has no choice."

"Would you take the rule of the Winter Court as Queen if you could?"

"Of course. The ruling of the Winter Court takes priority over anything else."

"Anything? Even your own happiness?"

I could feel the weight of his stare upon me.

I didn't reply.

"Surely you need to be happy to be a good ruler. Surely you need to know love to know how to love your kingdom. Your mother loved. Even if she turned her back on it in the end."

I sighed and Isaac took that cue to change the subject. "So according to your sister's diary, last night she went to the cinema and Billy kissed her. And that's where you'll be picking up from today."

"I can't kiss him! I've never even met him!"

Isaac shrugged his shoulders. "You volunteered for this task."

I mumbled under my breath some choice words about my sister. Then I felt guilty.

"You might as well enjoy yourself while you're saving lives." Isaac laughed.

"And what will you be doing while I'm out with my new boyfriend?" I asked him.

"Me? I have a date with the Xbox. That's one thing

I do miss when I'm not down here on Earth. Now go and make yourself look pretty before your boyfriend texts you. Which he will as soon as he's awake."

Isaac was right. By the time I'd showered, found something to wear, and fixed my hair, there was a text on my phone.

Billy: Want to come over? Aaron and Mum are at work. I could make you breakfast.

My stomach roiled having just eaten. I wasn't brave enough to see him yet. I needed more time.

Thea: Actually, I didn't sleep well last night and I've woken with a headache. Raincheck for later?

Billy: You sure you're not blowing me off?

The language of these people still looked strange to me, even though I understood it.

. . .

Thea: No! I really do have a headache. I can meet you later?

Billy: Okay. Ring me later. Feel better soon.

Thea: Thank you xo

I crawled back underneath the covers of my bed. What with the nightmare and the early start, I really could use a nap. My eyes closed as I imagined my lips touching those of someone I'd only yet seen in a dream. But the eyes I imagined as I closed my own, weren't Billy's, but rather the cold ones that had met mine through a window.

CHAPTER SEVEN

Mercy

After Isaac had read me the riot act about how avoidance would not rescue my sister, I apologised to him yet again, texted Billy, and set off for his house. I stopped at the end of the street and looked over once again at where he lived. This was it. From now on I was Leatha, not Mercy. I had to remember to be the wild rose of my sister, not the tame snowdrop I was.

Billy opened the front door as I walked up the path.

"I got Infinity War for us to watch. Plus coke and popcorn."

Coke? He wanted to give me drugs?

"I'll leave the coke to Aled if it's okay with you." I told him.

He burst into laughter. "Good one."

I followed him inside, not knowing what was so amusing. Until I saw the soda bottle and remembered it was called Coca-Cola. Coke. Oh, thank the goddess that's what he meant.

I wandered past all the family photos on the mantle-shelf. He and his brother at various stages of their lives. A couple of photos had their mother on too. There were none of their father.

I couldn't ask him about them because he may have already told my sister.

"Thea. Hey, Earth calling Thea."

I realised he was talking to me. She called herself Thea? I guess Leatha was an unusual name for here, but I'd read some magazines. There were worse things to be called.

"Yeah? Sorry, I was miles away."

"Yeah, thinking about Thor no doubt."

I smiled. "Something like that."

Billy gestured to the sofa, and I took a seat. He came to sit at the side of me and pulled the coffee table closer so our drinks and popcorn were in reach.

"I think that's us all set? You ready?" He asked.

"Sure."

He pressed play, and we sat back. About thirty

minutes through the film he grabbed hold of my hand. I jumped a little at first.

"Sorry." He said, taking his hand away.

I retook it in mine. "It's okay. I was just so busy watching the movie it took me by surprise."

He smiled at me. I could see why my sister liked him. He seemed a nice guy. I liked feeling how warm his hand was in my own.

We watched the rest of the film and when the credits came up, I excused myself to visit the bathroom while Billy re-filled our glasses.

We sat on the sofa chatting. "If you're free tomorrow, we could go to the cafe and meet some of the others?"

I bit my lip. "Do you think Aled will turn up?"

"Who knows. No one's seen anything of him since the fire. He's probably grounded, or working all the hours god sends to pay his parents back for the cost of the damage."

The door banged, and I heard an expletive from the hallway.

A tall guy came through the door. All dark hair and matching mood. He looked at me with a pinched expression. "Can you not discard your shoes in the hallway, Thea? I just nearly broke my neck."

"Aaron. Leave her alone."

"Sorry." I said. "I'll remember for next time."

"Yeah, you said that last time." He pushed past the television and headed for the kitchen. "Where's Mum?"

"She's gone to see Gran. Due back anytime."

A kettle was switched on. Billy got up from the sofa. "I'm going to take a leak. Ignore Aaron if he moans at you."

"I will." I said and smiled.

When he'd gone, I looked at my watch. Thankfully, I could go home now. I'd done one evening in the life of my sister, though I was still no closer to finding out what went wrong.

As soon as the door closed behind Billy, Aaron came into the room. His eyes burned with dislike. "What were you doing on our road so early this morning? You don't live around here."

I decided to deny all knowledge.

"I wasn't on your road this morning. I was tucked up safely in bed."

That made him falter for a moment, his eyes scrunching up.

Billy returned and sat back next to me on the sofa. "I'd better walk you to the bus stop. One more week and I'll be hopefully be able to drive you home."

The vision of him pumping the brakes flashed into my mind and I flinched.

"Hey, my driving's not that bad. No need to look so worried."

I was about to say something but then lights shone through the living room window.

"Mum's home." Billy said.

My heart seemed to fall into my shoes. First Aaron, and now I had to meet Billy's mum, someone else I'd already supposedly met. How would Leatha talk to her?

I pasted a smile on my face as she came through the door.

"Oh, hey, Thea."

"Hey, Mrs B."

"I've told you to call me Dawn how many times now? I thought we were past this."

"Sorry, Dawn. Could I make you a cup of tea? Aaron just boiled the kettle."

By the look Aaron and Billy gave me, I could tell I'd made another error. Come on, Mercy. When did Leatha do anything like that? She was a princess through to her core. Diva all the way.

Dawn stared at me a second.

"I mean it won't take you two seconds to get another mug out for your mum will it, Aaron?" I quickly interjected. "Right, I'm going to get off home. Billy's taking me to the bus stop."

"Okay. Night, Thea." Dawn said.

After gathering my shoes, I left the house with Billy. As I walked past his mother's car I gasped. This was the one. The car from my nightmares. His mother's car. *So maybe if I did something to break her car, I could stop what happens?* Billy grabbed hold of my hand. I'd have to discuss this with Isaac when I got home.

Billy held my hand all the way to the bus stop. Now what happened? I couldn't get on a bus. I'd have no idea where I was going.

He pulled me towards him and his lips touched mine. They were soft and warm. "I've been wanting to do that again all night." He told me.

I smiled shyly and then remembered I was Thea, so I pulled him back towards me and planted my lips firmly on his. He moved his head, tilting it; our mouths parted and our tongues tangled.

But I felt nothing other than sorry that Leatha wasn't experiencing the kiss meant for her.

We broke apart when Billy announced my bus was arriving. There was nothing coming at all, but he walked away convinced he'd seen me onto the bus.

I waited a while and then I retraced my steps back down the road until I was on my way back to the house.

Once back on a familiar street, I breathed a sigh of relief.

"I knew it." A voice boomed from behind me. "Some really weird shit is going on and you have something to do with it, Thea Queen."

I whisked around to find Aaron Buckley standing there. His arms were wrapped across his chest showing me he meant business, meant to challenge me. His grey eyes pierced me like a sharp corner of a stone. Destiny had sent me a curve ball.

"What are you talking about? You sound deranged." I cocked my hip and placed a hand on it as I'd seen Leatha do so many times in a strop.

He walked forward with intent until he was right next to me, looking down into my eyes. He took my chin in his hand and tilted it up, making my brown gaze meet his steely one. There was something in that gaze though, something familiar as if this wasn't only the second time I'd stared into those eyes.

"Either I'm going insane or there are things happening lately, I have no logical explanation for." He said, his voice scarily calm. Like a steady ocean before a shark blasts through the water.

"Last night, I drove my mum to the hospital where we identified Billy's body." He said. "This morning the calendar says it's four days earlier than the day I was on, and my brother is very much alive."

I stood silent and still.

"I followed you to the bus stop and watched as Billy left you there. He waved like you'd got on one, and then you walked away, and here you are walking around the corner from where we live."

I brazened it out. "So I lied about where I live. I'm not from a wealthy family. I just live around the corner."

"But I gave you a lift home last week, Thea, and it took me twenty minutes to reach your house. The house I can now see in my eyeline. So am I mad or is something inexplicable going on?"

"You're deranged. I said it already." I knocked his hands away from my chin and started to walk down the street.

"If I'm crazy, then it will get worse in every area of my life and I'll seek psychiatric help." He shouted after me. "If I'm not crazy, then my brother dies on Friday night. If I'm not crazy, then you have to help me save him, Thea Queen."

I was ready to run back to the house, to ask Isaac for help, but instead I stopped and turned back around to Aaron.

"My name isn't Thea Queen." I told him. "I'm her twin sister, Princess Mercy Northcote of the Winter Court in Andlusan."

His mouth dropped into a sneer.

"You asked for the truth. There it is. Now you can decide if you're insane or if something illogical is going on. Now it's late and I'm tired. I shall spend tomorrow trying to work out what happened before your brother's fatal car accident. If you decide you believe me, and you haven't booked yourself into an institution by then, meet me at the front bench of Saunders Park at nine pm."

Then I did turn and walk away. I needed to speak to Isaac urgently about this turn of events.

CHAPTER EIGHT

Aaron

The facts were that when I went to work everything played out with a sense of déjà vu. I just knew I'd had this day before. The weirdest thing was I knew Louisa Scott threw boiling hot coffee on me on Friday and yet at this moment in time she was still texting me trying to get me to take her out again.

It really was enough to have me thinking I'd gone insane. My only chance of the truth, I knew, rested with Thea Queen. I couldn't explain why I knew that. I just did.

Then I got home from work to find her in my house, having spent the evening watching a film with my brother. But the Thea in our room was not the one I'd met before. Once again her eyes weren't cold and calculating, and her manner had been totally different. She'd seemed almost shy. How could Billy not notice?

Because you're insane?

There was only one thing to do.

Follow her.

I slipped out of the back door. My mother had gone to get ready for bed. I hung around in a shop doorway until Billy said goodbye and walked away from Thea at the bus stop. When he was out of view, she turned and started to walk down the street. She was so intent on where she was going that she never noticed the person behind her. Not until I challenged her.

I don't know what I'd expected her to say, but it certainly wasn't some bullshit about being a Princess and Thea's sister.

Having decided I was insane and I'd call the psychiatrists first thing in the morning, I'd stopped when on my way back home I'd recalled something she'd said.

'I shall spend tomorrow trying to work out what happened before your brother's fatal car accident.'

I had only said he died on Friday. I'd never told her how.

She could bet her life I'd be in Saunders Park tomorrow at nine.

CHAPTER NINE

Mercy

"How's your evening been?" Isaac asked me moments after I'd walked through the door, kicked my shoes off, and collapsed onto the sofa.

"Complicated." I sat up. "Something strange happened tonight, Isaac. Billy's brother, Aaron. He knows Billy died."

Isaac frowned. "What? How?"

I shrugged my shoulders.

"He followed me after I left Billy and he said weird shit was going on and Thea was connected to it. He added illogical things were happening, or he was going insane and he said he knew Billy had died on Friday. That he'd been with his mum to identify the body."

Isaac scrubbed a hand through his hair. "This

shouldn't be possible. Time should have rewound back for everyone. What did you say? You put him off right? Told him he was crazy."

"Yeah."

Isaac exhaled. "Thank God. I'll look into why this could have happened and how we reset his memory."

I chewed on my bottom lip.

Isaac's glance shot to me, his lips flattening. "What did you do, Mercy?"

"Well, after I told him he was deranged, I then told him who I really was."

His eyes widened. "You did what?"

"It's okay. Then he thought I was deranged."

Isaac clutched at his hair. "Why would you do that?"

"Because he *does* know something's not right, and he *does* know his brother dies. Maybe he can help somehow? Anyway, I said if he chose to believe me he could meet me at Saunder's Park tomorrow evening. He works in the day, and tomorrow I need to carry on Thea's life as it happened, not have Aaron Buckley changing things."

Isaac's mouth twisted to the side. "I don't like this, Mercy. We don't know this guy at all."

"He just wants to save his brother, Isaac. Just as I want to save my sister. How can I deny him what I'm so desperate to do myself?"

He exhaled. "Okay, well just be careful. We'll work tonight on a spell where you can cloak yourself if need be, so you won't be seen. That way no one else can follow you home."

"Thank you." I felt like I needed to break up the tension now in the room. "Hey, I know it's pretty late, but I fancy trying a pizza. Shall I call in an order? I figure I should live a little while I'm on this adventure."

Isaac stared at me. "I read what she put in her diary. The dig at you being serious and no fun. Don't feel guilty for who you are, Mercy. Don't feel you have any points to prove."

I sighed. "Maybe she was right. I live my tidy ordered life, doing what's expected of me. It's all I've ever done. My duty. Maybe I should loosen up a little. Surely I can do my duty and have a little fun?"

Aaron smirked. "So what do you want on your pizza?"

∼

I woke the next morning, and I just knew some things. That on my phone would be a text saying to meet at the cafe at lunchtime. I knew a few of the gang had summer jobs and so I saw different people at different times. That no one ever questioned why I didn't work. Billy only worked on a weekend at a fast-food joint.

His mum thought it was good he had some down time. I woke knowing that out of the girls in the gang: Marie, Carly, and Saffron, I was closer to Marie. She would be there at lunch.

After a shower, I ate breakfast with Isaac, and then I had my lessons in the study of the art of witchcraft. I was trying not to dwell too much on anything that was happening in my life, but rather just work with it. Practicing witchcraft, travelling through time, and living on Earth were a lot to comprehend. It was better I went along as if in a dream, taking each day as it passed.

"So now you've spent a day or two here, do you think you'll miss it when you go back home?" Isaac interrupted my thoughts.

I shook my head.

"No. My home is most definitely Andlusan. I like the meadows, the slower pace of life. My family home. Here I am uncomfortable. I want to put a gown back on. I hate these scratchy trousers."

"And if you rescue your sister, will she be happy to return to Andlusan? What if she wants to stay here?"

"Well, she cannot. Her place is at home ruling Andlusan. She will have had her adventures and hopefully learned from them. She has put not only her own life in danger, and Billy's, but ours too. What if our travel had gone awry?"

I looked at the clock. "Oh Goddess! I must get to

the cafe." I smacked my palm into my forehead. "Isaac. I forgot with everything I had to tell you last night. The car I dream of. It's Billy's mother's car. So surely if we stop it from working, then Billy cannot drive it and crash?"

"Hmmmm, definitely something to think about. A very good option. I will ponder it while you go enjoy yourself with your friends."

"They aren't my friends. They're *Thea's* friends. I air-quoted my sister's Earth name.

"But right now you're Thea, remember? So go have fun." Isaac made a shooing motion.

"Okay, I'm going."

∽

At lunch there was me, Billy, Marie, and Billy's mate, Tom. We ordered pizza and garlic bread to share, and I had a coke. I loved the taste of some of this food although it couldn't beat the hearty stews of home. All three of them were great fun, and I found myself genuinely enjoying their company. It made me think of how back home I only spent time with my sister and with our ladies-in-waiting. When I returned perhaps it was time to make a few friends? The problem was at home you couldn't trust if people were genuine or friendly because of your position.

The guys went to play on the pool table at the back of the room and Marie slid in alongside me at my side of the booth.

"So how's it going with you and Billy?"

I smiled. "I like him."

"Well, I know that, duh? Did you get in there and get a snog?"

I felt my cheeks heat. It was difficult to act like my sister.

"He kissed me after the cinema, and last night walking home."

"You lucky bitch. Billy Buckley. He's held our hearts for some time. Just needed the right girl to come along." She sighed. "Well, me and Tom had a heavy make-out session last night."

"How far did you get?" My mouth said, completely out of my control. I'd not thought this sentence, not prepared to say these words. Maybe they just had to be said, to move things into fate's alignment?

"We got very handsy. Let's put it that way." Marie smiled. "And he is very good with them."

"Did you feel it then?" Again, my mouth ran away without me. Bloody Thea!

"Well, yeah, course. Hey, you're not a virgin are you, Thea? You've been around a man before?"

"Yeah, course. I was just showing interest in the

fact you are getting handsy with Tom and I wanted to know if he had a gigantic dick."

I started coughing. How on earth could I stop Thea's words from pouring out of my mouth? I'd never heard language like it. But the important part came next. The thought passed through my head.

I must sleep with Billy. I must know what it is like to lie with a man.

∼

After we'd eaten, Marie and I went around the clothes and accessories shops on the high street. Billy had football practice that night and I'd told him I'd catch up with him tomorrow. I saw a dress I liked, a maxi dress which I felt much more at home in. Marie encouraged me to buy it. When I opened my purse, there was a credit card to put my purchases on. I wondered how much of the store, magic would allow me to buy.

I realised I knew the answer. Isaac was teaching me well. I would be able to get what I needed to do the task I had come here to do. No more. I felt more comfortable in the dress so I could get it. The question was, how had Thea got things, because none of her being here was for a selfless purpose.

I soon got the answer.

"How come you paid today? It's much more fun

when you walk out of the changing rooms with something on under your clothes. You're my hero, you know that, right? These companies can afford to lose a few things with how much they overcharge."

I quickly masked my alarm that my sister had been stealing. "Yeah, well I'd have a bit of a task trying to sneak a maxi out, wouldn't I?"

"Fair point. Okay, I'd better head home. Catch you later, Thea." She hugged me outside the door of the shop and left.

I sagged in relief that I'd managed to get through lunch and the afternoon and headed off in what I knew was the direction of home.

But partway back, I felt a pull to walk in another direction. I walked for a long time until houses got closer together, and there was as much furniture outside the houses as there was inside. Abandoned mattresses and sofas rotted in gardens. Gangs of little kids scooted and biked around, their language filthy. But my feet walked me right up to one of the doors and I rang the bell.

Aled Davies answered the door. His blonde hair looked like it needed a wash. Dark circles underneath and bruising above made his blue eyes look haunting, amplifying the whites.

"What happened to your face?"

He rolled his eyes. "Oh, Thea, darlin'. Concerned

now, are ya? Why's that? Looking for some gear and reckoning I might have replaced my stock by now?"

"No. I just wondered—"

"Do you care?" He sneered. "Only I've been told that while I've been lying low, you've been getting close to our Billy. I said you were a prick tease; did you only kiss me to get some free shit?"

"Are you in danger?"

He cackled with hysterical laughter. "I owe my supplier two grand. When I couldn't make the first payment, he did this." He pointed to his eyes. "Now I have the first payment, but I don't have the second, so fuck knows what he's going to do next. He did threaten to set the rest of my house on fire, so there's that."

I quickly opened my purse to see if there was anything in it to give him to help. It was empty apart from a few pound coins; yet in the cafe and shops I knew I had carried much more. I wasn't able to help him. Fate said no.

"I only have these few pounds."

"Save them. There's nowhere near enough. Buy a couple of flowers to put on my grave instead, hey? Now if there's nothing else, you can go."

"But—"

"What do you want, Thea? Why are you here? You blow hot and cold and I don't know where I am with you." He moved closer to me and stroked his hand down my face. "I've told you I want you. I think about you all the time. But I won't share. I'm not a good man, Thea. I fight dirty to get what I want."

A car pulled up at the kerb.

"Fuck." Aled pushed me away from him and slammed the door shut. I heard the lock click.

The man exited the car. He was a tall thin man with white-blonde hair. He wore a suit, and a thick gold bracelet dangled from his wrist. He wolf-whistled at me.

"Well, what have we here? You Aled's bit of fluff?"

I swallowed. "I'm just a friend. I came to see how he was doing because we've not seen him for a while."

"Yeah, funny that. I've not seen him for a while either. When I knock at his door, he doesn't answer. You watch, it'll happen again now." He knocked, and sure enough Aled ignored it.

The man grabbed hold of my arm so hard I swore it would cause bruises.

"Seeing as he seems to have time for you, you tell him this from me." He bent right down near to my face. "I want my money. He has until Saturday and then I get serious. Unless you'd like to pay off some of his debt?" He stroked a hand down my body. Closing my eyes, I called upon my goddesses and thought words of protection. I felt a swarm of heat and then the man staggered back, staring at the hand he clutched in his other one. "I'm burned. My hand's burned. What the fuck did you do, bitch?"

I held my hand in front of me and flames licked at my fingers. "Get away from me." I spat.

"I don't know what trick you're pulling but tell him this." He jabbed his fingers towards the house. "Saturday, or he's a dead man."

He got back in the car and drove away.

The flames died down from my fingertips, but I felt so thirsty.

I ran all the way home.

∽

"So your sister was involving herself with this Aled, but I don't see how any of that ties in to Billy stealing his mother's car and crashing it. Your dreams point to a joyride where he was egged on by your sister. The fact that you are saying words she said, means that you may well find yourself asking him to drive the car."

"What if I do that and can't say anything else? If I can't stop it?"

"There will be something we can do to change things. I'll go back through the books tonight and see if I can find anything that can stop your speech being hijacked. We're fighting against a fate that's already been changed. They weren't supposed to be in that car and that means that fate should allow us to change things back to the way they were meant to be."

"Why did she have to do this? It's too much, Isaac. My brain can't cope with all this."

"I was going to come with you tonight to see this Aaron, but we can't afford to waste time, so you go talk to him and I'll get the spell books out."

I was secretly relieved that Isaac wasn't coming with me to see Aaron. The last thing I needed was two men butting heads. I'd handle Aaron on my own. I knew from my encounter with the drug supplier that I could protect myself if necessary.

So after our evening meal, I dressed in my new maxi dress with a cardigan around my shoulders. I sprayed some of Thea's perfume on me, refusing to acknowledge why I was doing so, and then I walked towards the park.

CHAPTER TEN

Aaron

I wasn't sure if she'd show up, but when I arrived at the park at five minutes past nine, she was there next to the bench; looking furtively around and pulling her cardigan closer over her chest.

Her shoulders visibly relaxed when she saw me.

"You okay?" I asked searching her face for answers.

"Yeah, it's just I'm not used to being alone in parks. There are a lot of places people could hide, aren't there?"

"I guess so, but I've never heard of any crimes being reported here. I wouldn't have agreed to meet you here if I'd thought it wasn't safe."

"Well, back home, I only go out with two bodyguards in tow, so this, being in Hallbridge, is all rather strange and taking some getting used to."

I nodded over the road. "There's a bar. Shall we go there? It should be pretty quiet on a Wednesday evening. Might not be as many midges around." I added as she wafted across her face for the second time since I'd stood there.

"Okay. I've not been in a bar before. Do they sell coke? The drink that is, not the drug?"

"You really aren't Thea, are you? You're nothing like her."

She sucked on her top lip.

"Thea isn't Thea either. Her name is Leatha. She's three minutes older than me, and three times as much trouble."

"Okay." I nodded my head. "I'm going to let you explain everything. I'm going to ask questions, and not assume that either you or I are suffering a mental breakdown. I guess that's the only way I'm going to get through this evening."

Her dark brown doe eyes met mine. "If it's any consolation, I'm way out of my comfort zone and keep pinching my own cheeks to make sure I'm actually here."

I reached over and pinched her cheek.

"Ow."

"Looks like you're here and this is real after all."

LAST RITES

I found a table in the corner. "You go sit down and I'll get you that coke. The drink, not the drugs." I teased. As I'd thought, the pub was quiet enough that we'd be able to talk undisturbed, but busy enough that there was a low hum of voices and we wouldn't be overheard.

Drinks in front of us, I went in my jacket pocket and took out three packets of crisps. "Beef, cheese and onion, and ready salted. Didn't know if you'd tried any yet. Not sure what you eat where you come from. Where is it you're a princess of, anyway?"

"I'm from the Winter Court in Andlusan."

"What's it like there? Describe it to me. Tell me who you are and why you're here. Why your sister was here. Is she from Earth?" I pulled at my hair. "Sorry for all the questions. I just don't know what's real anymore."

Her tongue darted out and licked across her top lip and I tried not to be fascinated. Thea was beautiful but I'd not been attracted to her cold nature. Mercy's warmth and her different mannerisms were making me take note. I needed to stop staring at her sweeping tongue and concentrate. She took a sip of her drink.

"The Winter Court is as it sounds. In Andlusan there are Courts for Spring, Summer, Autumn, and Winter, and as you'd expect the Courts are as described. We have snow, ice. It is very beautiful, but very cold. You acclimatise though if it's all you've ever known. I don't travel often to the other Courts. We're all pretty much self-sufficient."

"This must be very different then? It's summer here. Flowers, sunshine, heat, a lot less clothing."

Instinctively she played with the strap of her dress. "Yes, it's most unusual."

"Sorry, you were saying..."

"Our mother died a month ago, leaving my sister next in line to the throne as she is three minutes older than me."

"I'm sorry for your loss."

She nodded. "Thank you. Leatha hates the royal side of things. She doesn't want to be Queen. I had no idea that she had been travelling the planes though until we found her in her room suffering. Our royal physician told me what had happened to her." She stared at me. "I know you are questioning your sanity. It's the same for me. I was told I come from a family of royal witches. That my mother banned witchcraft because it killed my father. I found this out only just before I travelled here at the start of the week. I'm completely out of my depth. If it wasn't for Isaac, I don't know what I would have done."

"Isaac?"

"He's a sorcerer. A warlock. He's had to hide in the

outskirts of the Winter Court to practice his craft. The royal physician put me in touch with him and he has been teaching me my craft, clearing me of the binds that had not allowed magic to run through my veins. He has travelled with me here to aid me in rescuing my sister."

"He's here?"

For some reason I didn't like the thought that Mercy was spending time with another man. I decided not to question my reasons for this. She was already kind of dating my brother.

"Yes. To anyone else he appears to be my brother. We're not sure why this is not working on you. It works on everyone else."

"What does? The magic?"

"Yes, it weaves stories, so no one questions my appearance here. I came here knowing many things like what a mobile phone is and how to work it. Sometimes I utter words that my sister must have said in the days leading up to the accident. Mostly though I sit wondering how long it will be before I can return home."

"You'll go back?" I felt an inward panic at the thought of her leaving. What the hell was wrong with me? I didn't know this woman. But as I gazed into her brown eyes, I felt like I had known her a long while. I shook myself. It wasn't possible. Then again everything happening here tonight didn't seem possible either.

"Yes. The Winter Court is my home. I belong there. Sometimes I think it would have been a lot easier if I had been born first. I've ended up acting like it my whole life anyway. Always the responsible one while Leatha does what the hell she likes." A hint of anger flared in her eyes, the first time I'd seen any fire within her.

"That doesn't seem fair. Though surely, you've had opportunity to be spontaneous yourself at times. Are you sure you've not just hidden behind your sister, living a safe life?"

The anger flared again.

"I say that because I know that's exactly what I've done." She sat back watching me. "My brother is the wild one. He'll go abseiling, drive quad bikes, drink underage. My dad left when I was young, so I grew up being told I was the man of the house. It stuck. Sometimes I wonder if I'm Billy's brother or father. I know it drives him insane that I'm always on his case. So you see, we aren't so different after all."

"I guess not." She narrowed her eyes. "So what you're saying is we're the boring ones? And that's partly through circumstance, but also—and I've been thinking of this while I've been here—through choice, through keeping ourselves small."

"Well, you could have an entirely fascinating life in Andlusan, but I work in a sports shop and yes my life is very, very dull."

"I like where I live, but yes, I could use a little more excitement in my life." Mercy smiled. "But it's Leatha being too impulsive that's led me here, so I'm kind of wary."

"So tell me how she got here. How you got here."

"I had a nightmare. That I was in a car and it crashed. Then I was standing at the side of the road and a man was telling me he was dying. I was too, and I saw a portal and jumped into it, saying I'd save him, I'd be back. But I wasn't me. I was my sister." She touched her face, above her lip. "I have a mole right here. Other than that we are more or less identical in our faces. We have a few differences elsewhere..." She trailed off, her cheeks pinking. "That's all I thought it was. A nightmare. But I was called to my sister's chambers, and that's where I was told she'd been travelling and that she was trapped."

"Trapped?"

"Yes, she's stuck in the planes between here and home because she caused the death of your brother. Leatha was not supposed to be here, and your brother was not fated to die. She's changed the future. When she created the portal to return home, she became trapped, because until what she did is fixed, she cannot move on." Mercy wiped a tear away from under her eye. "In three days time at home, it's Leatha's coronation. If I don't have her back on that date, the spell put upon her to protect her will break. Then the royal physician will perform the Last Rites and she will die. By causing the death of your brother on earth, she has to die. For balance. That's why I am here. To correct whatever my sister did, to right her wrongs, so that your brother lives and therefore my sister does too."

"So we need to find out what she did. Do you have any clues?"

"Only that Billy took your mother's car. I know that Leatha had been experimenting with drugs and had crossed paths with a guy called Aled."

"Aled Davies? He's bad news."

"I know. I met him yesterday. Leatha did something that lost him his supply of merch. His supplier threatened him with harm yesterday. I was there. My body steered me towards him so I was meant to be there, to see it. I don't know if it's connected. Aled kissed Leatha before Billy. He's jealous that she's choosing your brother."

"Do you think she's serious about Billy?"

She shrugged her shoulders. "I don't know. My guess is that Leatha has been like an escaped prisoner, trying everything to celebrate her freedom. We have been protected from romance in Andlusan as we are supposed to marry for the good of the Court. Leatha's diary suggested that she liked your brother a lot, but she'd only been here a few weeks."

"She left a diary? Doesn't that tell you what happened?"

"Unfortunately not. Pages of it are blank. Isaac says it's because there are things we have to work out for ourselves."

Once again, I bristled at the name. "So what's in it for this Isaac? Why is this stranger helping you?"

"Because if I save Leatha and we acknowledge our witch heritage, he and his family can come out of hiding and be free."

"Are you sure he doesn't want to impress you or Leatha so he can become a Prince?"

"How dare you?" Mercy snapped. "Isaac has been nothing but generous with his time. He came highly recommended from Lord Thomas who is like an uncle to me. He is becoming like a cousin."

I wondered how this Isaac would feel about being likened to a cousin because I wouldn't have liked it one little bit. *God, stop it! Stop these stupid thoughts. You're here to listen and try to save your brother's life. Embrace the crazy.* All I needed now was to see proof.

"Can you show me a little of your craft?"

Her eyes widened, and her mouth dropped open. "I don't know. I'm not very experienced."

"We could go back to the park, now it's dark. I think I believe you, but I just know if I saw something that was beyond Earth, it would help me."

She nodded her head, knocked back her drink and stood up.

"Come on then. Before I change my mind."

CHAPTER ELEVEN

Mercy

This should have all felt awkward.

Here I was spending time with a man I barely knew, while I was unaccompanied.

All unknown terrain, and yet I was chartering it with aplomb. I could surmise it was being in Thea's body making me feel more comfortable given her confidence, but I didn't feel deep down in my soul it was that at all. Deep down I knew I liked Aaron Buckley even though I barely knew him.

We'd heard stories about love, about soulmates. Our mother had said our father had been hers. That part of her had died when he had. Perhaps that's why she had always been closed off and businesslike. I'd assumed it was because she was Queen, but maybe it was because she was protecting herself from it happening again?

Moving through the darkness further into the park should have made me tense with the potential danger. But as I turned to look at Aaron, he smiled, and I instantly relaxed.

"Here?" I pointed towards the foot of a large oak tree.

"Okay." Aaron walked towards it, removed his jacket and placed it on the ground. "It might be damp." Was all he said as he gestured towards the jacket, indicating for me to sit there.

I lowered myself to the ground, aware that his jacket only covered a small space. As he sat alongside me, the side of his body touched mine, causing goosebumps to rise along my arms. I shivered.

"Are you cold? Do you want to put my jacket on instead?" He asked.

"No. It's fine. Wait and watch. I just need a moment of quiet, please?"

"Okay."

I crossed my legs and placed my hands over my knees.

"Are we meditating?" Aaron interrupted.

I opened my eyes and glared at him. "If you interrupt me, you might end up turned into a frog, so can you let me concentrate?"

"Sorry, I guess I'm just nervous." He admitted.

"Well don't be. I got the basics covered."

I spoke a protection spell and then I opened my eyes and called to the elements until a small fire danced on the ground in front of us. To anyone passing, it would look like I'd struck a match among abandoned twigs, but Aaron could see the truth of it, could see that I'd conjured it in front of us.

"I guess I should thank you for making us toasty warm?"

The light from the flames was reflected in his irises. He no longer looked at me with a flint gaze. He looked relaxed, and it suited him.

"Do you get along well with your brother?"

"Yes, despite the fact we're very different. There are only two years between us which helps."

"So you're nineteen?"

"Yes. How old are you?"

"Eighteen in Andlusan in three days time."

He looked blankly at me. "I don't understand."

"Time is standing still for me in Andlusan. So here I am three days before my eighteenth birthday for all the time I'm on this visit. When I return time will move on."

Aaron shook his head. "This is beyond weird."

"I know."

We sat in silence for a few moments watching the flames. Flames that didn't crackle as they really didn't exist.

"So Thea is to be crowned on your actual eighteenth birthdays?"

"Yes. We have had no ruler for the last month. Just advisors of our mother's who have helped things tick over. Andlusan is not a complicated place to rule, thankfully."

"Tell me more about it. What do you eat? How do you spend your days?"

I sat back against the bark of the tree. "I sleep in the most comfortable bed you could ever imagine, wrapped in many blankets because of the Winter. My lady-in-waiting gets me up and prepares me a warm bath. It soothes me and sets me up for the day. After breakfasting, usually on porridge and berries, I tend to do work for the Court, as my sister otherwise would leave it. Then lunch and more paperwork. Lunch is usually cured meats, along with leaves from our garden. We eat a hearty meal in an evening, mostly stews, and then my evening is my own. I mainly read, sometimes I do needlework. It's a quiet but satisfying life."

"So the only company you have is that of your

lady-in-waiting, Court officials, and your sister's company at mealtimes?"

"Oh, I dine alone. We have tables in our rooms. The dining rooms are only for official occasions. Once Leatha is crowned they will open once more and the sounds of dancing and merriment may once more be heard in the palace."

"You should not have to dine alone, Mercy. You are too special to be ignored."

I swallowed. His face was so close to mine that shadows of my body danced upon his skin due to the glow of the flames. My tongue darted out to sweep across my top lip as my mouth felt so dry.

And then he kissed me. His lips brushed mine, soft at first, and then they returned. His hand went behind my head, gathered in my hair, and he claimed my mouth with his own. Feelings I had never experienced before fired through my body. My body, not Leatha's. I held my hand up behind Aaron's head and could see my body like a haze over the top of my sisters. He had sparked my own essence with his kiss. Is this how it had felt when Leatha had kissed Billy? If so then I understood her reluctance to return home. It was like my body heated throughout and strange feelings passed through me, from my head to my toes.

Aaron broke the kiss and cleared his throat. "You-

you look different." He felt above my lip and I knew my mole was there.

"How is this possible? You're you... not her."

I shook my head. "I don't know. I'm not going to question it though. It feels good to be fully me for a while."

"I'm sorry. I shouldn't have done that." He looked at the ground and I realised the flames were no longer there.

That was because they were inside me. Licking my insides and talking to me.

More, more, more.

"Don't be sorry." I caught his confused gaze with my own more certain one. "I liked it. Kiss me again."

And he did. We kissed like our lives depended on it. Emotions swirled around me. Feelings I'd never experienced before. I craved more before it had even stopped.

Like burgers and ice cream.

That stopped me. My lips froze against his.

"We have to save them." I whispered.

"I know." He whispered back. "But give me tonight, Mercy. We don't know what will come tomorrow. If we'll ever be able to be together again. Tomorrow we battle for our siblings to live, but tonight please be mine."

I looked at him and nodded, and he laid me back against the ground and claimed my body as his own.

And as I laid there afterward, naked in his arms and content, I heard twigs snapping and male voices.

"So, that's twenty quid, okay? You want more, you text that same number, and I'll meet you here. Got to be off grid for a while. You know anyone wants any, give 'em my name. I need to make some money and fast. Anything anyone wants, DVD player, iPhone. Let me know and I'll get it for you."

One man's voice faded away along with his footsteps.

Then Aled Davies came into view. His hands unbuttoning the waistband of his jeans.

"Whoa. Sorry there, just wanted to pee. Didn't realise there were people here." I hid my face into Aaron's shoulder.

"Take a hike, mate. Can't you see I'm busy?" Aaron placed an item of clothing over us. I presumed it was my maxi-dress.

"Oh my god, is that you, Thea? Fucking hell, is no man safe around you? At least I know where I stand now." I cringed in Aaron's arms.

"Fucking your brother's girlfriend. Classy." A flash went off.

"I'll have a photo of this if you don't mind. It's going to cost you two grand for me to delete it though."

He walked away laughing, at the same time as tears ran from my own eyes onto Aaron's chest.

"Do a spell." Aaron said urgently.

"I don't know how." I snivelled. "Goddess, I don't know enough. I need Isaac." Sitting up, I quickly dressed myself. "I'm so stupid. I shouldn't have been doing this here with you. I should have been concentrating on saving my sister."

"Well, I regret nothing." Aaron said stiffly.

"Yeah, well we'd better hope that what we just did doesn't have repercussions." I spat. And then I ran. He didn't chase after me, just let me go.

I needed Isaac's help again. But how on earth was I going to explain what had happened?

When I got to the house Isaac wasn't in. Frustrated, I got into the shower, washing the smell of grass and Aaron off my body. But I couldn't wash away the feel of him, my memories of his touch on my skin. The ache in my core. I had bled slightly as we were told we would. I had given my innocence to a man from Earth. What had I been thinking?

You weren't thinking. I berated myself.

But the heat from the shower began to calm me and I realised that in doing what I had done that evening, I had begun to experience some of what my sister had been pursuing.

I was living my life.

And all of a sudden what Leatha had been rebelling against and fighting for made perfect sense to me.

She just wanted to live.

As I sat in front of the dressing table mirror and looked upon my reflection, I was back in Leatha's body once more.

To save that life.

CHAPTER TWELVE

Aaron

I ambled home, considering everything that had happened.

Seeing her spells.

Yet the main spell from her wasn't connected to witchcraft, just biology. It had not been my intention to sleep with her, yet that was exactly what I had done.

And it had been her. Her body had changed from that of her sister.

I'd made love with Mercy. Her essence, her soul, had shone through and responded to my every touch.

I needed to sleep. Needed time to process. Time to figure what to do with Aled Davies.

Because I didn't have two grand, and if I had it wasn't going to a drug dealer, petty thief, and low life.

I quietly slipped my key in the lock and opened the door. Then I tiptoed into the living room.

"Where've you been, Aaron?"

My mum was sitting on the sofa in the dark. I could see a glass of wine in her hand, the glass carrying the tiny reflection of the nearby streetlight.

"Just out with a friend." I told her. "We went to the Red Lion, then for a walk."

"Okay." She took a sip of her wine.

"Are you okay, Mum?" I sat down next to her on the sofa and looked at her face more closely. "Has something happened?"

She shrugged. "You just seem to not be yourself. You never sneak out of the house without saying where you are going. And then the other day, you were talking about a crash. Are you in trouble?"

"No." I put a hand on her arm. "Not at all. I'd had a terrible dream, a nightmare that Billy had taken your car and crashed it. It had been so real, Mum. But of course once I was properly awake, I realised it was just a dumb dream. And as for going out," I scratched the back of my head. "Bit embarrassing but I got a booty call. I decided to be a little more Billy, and a little less me."

"That's what I'm afraid of." She said.

I smirked. "Don't worry, I won't do anything too bad."

She finished her wine and stood up. "I guess I should head up now I know you're back. I have a big meeting at work tomorrow."

"Okay. Night, Mum." I stood up, leaned down, and kissed her forehead.

Her lips pressed together in a slight grimace.

"Mum, stop worrying."

"You smell of Thea." She said, then walked up the stairs leaving me standing there.

∼

What could I say to that?

I headed to the kitchen, spotted my mum's half-drunk bottle of wine and I finished off the rest of it at speed. Then slightly buzzed and tired, I went to bed myself, wondering vaguely what tomorrow would bring.

CHAPTER THIRTEEN

Mercy

Thursday morning.
The crash happened tomorrow. I was no nearer to stopping it.

Rather, I was nearer to causing it to happen. I'd made more of a mess. Sleeping with Aaron. Blackmailed by Aled. Next would be being scoffed at and scorned by Isaac.

I dressed and headed downstairs where I could hear him clattering around in the kitchen. Better I faced him now and got it over with.

"Do you want an omelette?" He quickly turned to me and asked before concentrating on the pan he was cooking eggs in.

"I'm not hungry." I walked over to the kettle. It

already held water, so I switched it on and put two spoonfuls of coffee in a mug. One wasn't going to cut it.

"How did your meeting with Aaron go?"

I let out a hearty sigh. "I fucked up, Isaac."

Isaac dropped the spatula, and it clattered noisily on the cooker top, remnants of egg splattering like bird poop on the silver surface.

"Sit."

Breakfast abandoned, Isaac pointed to the kitchen table. I poured boiling water in my mug, added a slosh of milk, and took the indicated seat.

"How?" Isaac looked me over like he was gathering evidence for a murder investigation.

I couldn't keep my eyes meeting his and I looked away.

"Oh my god, Mercy, what did you do?"

"I slept with him."

Isaac's hand banged down hard on the table making me flinch. "What? You only went to talk to him. How did that happen?" He scrubbed a hand through his hair. "Lord Thomas is going to kill me. With a look. Not even with a spell. Just a look will do it."

"What's this got to do with Lord Thomas?"

"He asked me to keep you safe. That's why I came with you."

"Sleeping with Aaron wasn't dangerous."

"No? What if his brother had seen you... Thea?"

"I'm not Thea."

He gestured at my body.

"It was strange, Isaac. My body became my own, but worse than that, Aled, the drug dealer, caught us and took photos. I had my head in Aaron's shoulder so it looked like Thea slept with him. Now he's blackmailing me."

"What?"

"He said if we didn't pay him two grand he'd show them to Billy."

Isaac sat in silence.

"Say something."

"We need to take care of this Aled guy. I'm going to finish my breakfast and get dressed. Then you can show me where he lives, and we'll see what we can do within the limits of allowable magic."

∼

So less than an hour later we were back at Aled's door. After much knocking, a curtain moved, and then footsteps drew nearer to the doorway. Finally, it opened and a smug-looking Aled stood back against the doorframe. "Brought my money, have you? Fast work, Thea... as usual." He nodded towards Isaac. "Big brother coming to bail you out then?"

"Can we come in?" Isaac said, while I remained silent. "I don't want to conduct business in the doorway."

Aled looked around, nodded, and we followed him inside.

The house was basic, but surprisingly clean. I guess it was judgemental of me to have thought that just because Aled sometimes appeared to forget basic hygiene of late, that his house would be the same.

Isaac took sage leaves out of his pocket. "Excuse me." He proceeded to light them and waft them in the air. Aled looked on fascinated. "Is this something new? What is it?"

"Isaac's a bit of a hippy." I lied, "so excuse him while he says some trippy things."

Isaac closed his eyes, the sage now having dripped dust all over the floor of Aled's living room.

With this sage, I cleanse the air
   And ask my Goddess for repair
   To put back that which was cast with ire
   Damaging property with the use of fire
   Please return to the way it was before
   As if magic had never been beyond this door.

. . .

The next thing I knew we were standing outside Aled's door.

"What the Goddess just happened?" I asked Isaac.

"Hopefully my spell worked. Which meant that Aled didn't lose his merch and now has no dealer after him."

"And so no longer wants to blackmail me, and is taken care of?"

"We can but hope."

"So what next?"

"You get on with your day, trying not to do anything that can set off catastrophic events. I suggest you spend the day with Billy like your sister would have done and avoid his brother. In fact, I think you need to tell Aaron that you made a mistake."

I nodded. My heart sank, but I knew he was right. Soon, with luck on our side, we would be gone from here, back to Andlusan. Aaron and Billy would be a distant memory from another time and place.

By tomorrow evening this would all be over one way or another.

"Isaac, if this doesn't work, can we come back again? Have another do-over."

He shook his head sadly. "I'm afraid not. If nothing changes then that's what fate has decided happens now, and we must live with the consequences."

I got a text from Billy.

Billy: Come over? We can go to the park later, but Mum is making me clean the house.

Me: Are you asking me to keep you company or help clean…?

Billy: I'd not thought of that. How good are you with a vacuum?

Me: Like the vacuum, I suck.

Billy: Oooh… that's a nice offer, but I have to clean, and Mum's home today.

Me: Oh my god. I did not just type that.

. . .

Billy: Lololololol.

My face had heated so much you could have fried an egg on each one of my cheeks. I said goodbye to Isaac who was now ensconced back in front of the Xbox and made my way to Billy's.

Sure enough, Dawn was there.

"Hey, Thea!" She smiled at me.

"Hi, Mrs—"

She put her hands on her hips, tilted her head and raised an eyebrow.

"Dawn."

"That's better. Now I don't feel one hundred years old. Now, sorry to spoil your plans but I've been asking him to help with chores all week, and nothing. So now I'm holding him captive until that room is done, and he's helped tidy the garage for me."

I shrugged. "It's fine. I agree he should help."

She switched on the kettle. "I'm just making a drink. Would you like one?"

"Yeah, could I have a coffee please? Any way it comes."

Dawn seemed really nice.

She chatted to me a little about school. I spoke using the knowledge that was just present in my head, pleased that I seemed to be managing to not create any suspicion. Billy had popped down to say hi, and that he wouldn't be much longer in his room. I agreed to help him clear out the garage. I figured it would pass the day on, and I quite liked organising things.

It was when I was completely off my guard that Dawn floored me with her words.

"So, which of my sons is it you're the most interested in, Thea? Because you aren't playing them both off, I can assure you."

I blanched.

"P-pardon?"

"Aaron came home last night smelling of your perfume, Thea. It's completely distinctive. In fact, I had been wracking my brains trying to place where it was from for weeks. It's been like trying to work through a fog to place it, but then, I remembered, and well, it set alarm bells ringing. What's it called again?"

I was lost for an answer to give her. It was sofella, a herb native to the Winter Court, mixed with vanoushka, a liquid pressed from the leaves of a Oosk tree. Somehow Leatha had brought it with her.

"I can't remember." I told her.

"Oh, I think you can. But what I really want to know is how you've got hold of a perfume that is not from here at all."

I looked up at her, attempting to read the expression on her face. She was guarded. We were like cat and mouse.

"How do you...?"

Fast as I said the words, she mumbled something under her breath and everything but us froze. The steam from my drink was paused in mid-air.

"Who are you?" She said.

I stared right back at her. "And who are you?"

"You first, while you're in my home causing friction between my sons. Aaron is saying strange things. Asking me about car crashes. Something is not right here."

I swallowed. "My name is Princess Mercy Elizabeth Northcote. I am from Andlusan."

Her eyes widened.

"And you know my perfume how?"

"I used to be called Lady Dawn Mandrake. I left Andlusan almost sixteen years ago."

My heart stuttered.

"Do you know Lord Thomas?"

She nodded. "I am... was... his wife."

"But, why...?" I was at a loss for words, but the ones she uttered next almost broke me.

"Mercy. I left because I killed your father... with magic."

CHAPTER FOURTEEN

Mercy

My ears were surely deceiving me?

Billy and Aaron's mum killed our father?

This couldn't be happening. I wished that Isaac were here to help me, but this time I was all on my own.

I'd never known what had truly happened to my father, so I figured I had nothing to lose by listening. Something was roiling within my body though. Some strange feeling I'd never had before. Like lightning through my veins. I felt like I would explode.

Closing my eyes, I mumbled a protection spell and calm came over me.

I turned my gaze upon Dawn. "I think you'd better

tell me about my father, and then I'll tell you why I'm here."

～

Dawn began. "I married Thomas in a handfasting ceremony in Andlusan. I had been your mother's lady-in-waiting and she and your father were both present at our wedding. I left my duties then and two years later I gave birth to Aaron. Your mother and I had known each other since we were children and that was why she'd chosen for me to be her lady-in-waiting. So when I left, we still spent time together. A few months after I discovered I was expecting Billy, your mother found out she was expecting you and your sister. I was able to reassure her throughout the pregnancy with it being my second."

She had a drink of her tea.

"We visited often, and as you began toddling you would follow Aaron everywhere. We found it highly amusing. He would bring you your favourite toys and cuddle you."

"So we met before? All those years ago?" Now I knew why he had felt familiar to me. Because I *had* known him before, even if I had been too young to remember it.

Dawn nodded.

"We had said in passing, your mother and I, that wouldn't it be wonderful should my sons marry her daughters. My husband was the royal physician, a Lord, but we knew that you were both destined to marry nobility from other Courts. Already some Courts were actively talking to your mother and father about future marriage to unite the Courts. I became paranoid that someone would harm my sons in order to remove them from their coveted position, friends of the current ruling Queen and her daughters."

Dawn fidgeted, scratching the back of her neck. "One day when Aaron was playing in the garden, he came back carrying a black rose. I asked him where he had got it from and he told me that a woman had given it to him in the garden. She had appeared, given him the flower, and had then disappeared again. The thorns from the stem of the rose had scratched his skin, and a rash was spreading through his body. Luckily, I knew a spell and it cleared as fast as it had come, but the threat was very real. They were saying they knew how to get to us. So, I told your mother that I would be unable to visit for the time being. That while ever there was a threat to my sons, I could not visit the palace. I became obsessed with setting up protection spells and magic around our own home, paranoid that someone would get in and harm my sons.

"Your father came to visit. I found out afterwards it

was to urge that I reconsider and take the boys to see you and Queen Violetta. I'd been busy in my kitchen and had not heard him approach. Billy screamed at the same time as fingers touched my shoulder and I let out a curse. Lightning went through your father's body and try as I might I couldn't save him."

By now, tears were running down Dawn's cheeks. "I thought he was an assassin. Billy had screamed because Aaron had taken his toy, but I didn't know that. I just heard his scream and felt hands on me."

She rubbed her eyes. "Your mother was inconsolable. She said she never wanted to see me again, and she banned magic and witchcraft in all forms. It was never to be spoken of again. I didn't feel like I wanted to live, but I had two sons that needed me. Thomas said we would live in exile, and we agreed we would travel to Earth and set up home here. But you got ill with a fever and were close to death. Violetta demanded my husband cure you, and said he owed her, *we owed her* for the fact she had lost one love of her life. She couldn't lose any more. She said Thomas was to stay as the Royal Physician, but I was not welcome. That she was yet to decide whether she would have me arrested for what I had done.

"So Thomas made the decision that I would live here on Earth with the boys, and he would stay in Andlusan. This satisfied your mother. The boys were no longer able to spend time with you, and I had then lost my husband—a rightful punishment for her losing hers.

"When we came here, I vowed I would never use magic or my craft again. Fate let us stay and I believe that was why. I changed relatively little here on Earth, just added to the population like many people do anyway. This now, freezing time, is the first time I have used magic in almost sixteen years."

I sat there frozen, trying to process everything Dawn had just told me.

We had known Aaron and Billy when young.

I needed to ask Isaac if Lord Thomas knew who Leatha had been visiting.

"Say something, Mercy, please." Dawn begged.

"I think fate has decided our families should meet again." I told her.

∼

I explained about Leatha's travels and why I was there. She cried as she learned of the crash that had claimed the life of her youngest son, but that we hoped we could rewrite. Tears fell at news of the death of my mother as Dawn told me that she'd missed my mum's friendship beyond comprehension.

It was clear that Dawn had lived for her sons. They

were the most precious thing in the world to her. But also, she had punished herself every single day for her involvement in my father's death. She'd gone to work as a nurse, so she could help save the lives of others as she'd been unable to save my father's, but she struggled with depression, when the blackness of what she'd done, the dark dog, visited her with its barking reminders.

"Dawn. It's clear what happened with my father was an accident." I told her.

"Mercy. That is kind of you to say, but you weren't there. I could be lying to you."

"Well, we'll see, shall we?"

I waved at the air and images from long ago appeared and while Dawn busied herself cleaning dishes, I watched what had happened that fateful day.

"Dawn. My father had crept up on you. He thought to make you jump. He was full of mischief that day."

She turned to me. "How can you know that?"

"I can hear his thoughts."

"Blessed goddess. Only the strongest of witches can hear the thoughts of a person who passed."

"Really?"

She nodded. "The magic is strong in you."

"I know little of it. Only what my friend Isaac has shown me. But I think it may be time for it not to be banished any more. As long as it is primarily used for good."

"But your mother…"

"My mother was scared. She lost her husband and didn't want to lose her daughters. But that fear stopped her from living her life. Fear has been stopping me from living mine. It cannot win. Anyway, like you say, fate is at play here, so are we not puppets at her service anyway?"

"So what do we do next?" Dawn said.

"Next, I help Billy tidy a garage, and we do what we can to make sure he avoids travelling in a car with me tomorrow. Isaac will render your car useless tomorrow morning. Other than that we can only be cautious and see how the day plays out."

She nodded. "I'll take the day off work, and between us we'll keep our eye on him at all times. I can't lose my son."

"And I can't lose my sister."

~

She un-froze the room and looked at me. "You know you could have overpowered me at any time, don't you? Your powers are far greater than mine. I can feel it within you."

"I'm nervous to use that I know little about. Isaac

has been teaching me, but I have only known of my own magic for days."

"Well, should you need them, don't be scared to call upon your powers. Your body will know the way. Just let it guide you."

"What about Lord Thomas? He is the other side of a travelling spell. Will you go to see him? Reconcile?"

She shook her head. "I'm not thinking of anything until I know my sons are safe and then I'll consider the future."

∼

I spent the afternoon helping to clear the garage and then Dawn made us something to eat. I left before Aaron was due home. Back at the house I told Isaac everything I'd learned today, asking him the question I strongly needed the answer to.

"Did Lord Thomas mention his wife and children? Did he know that's where Leatha had travelled?"

"He never said a word. I genuinely think he has no idea. Looks like Leatha travelling the planes has set the potential in motion for a lot of things to be solved."

"What, fate sent her to Earth so she could get Lord Thomas re-united with his family?"

"No, idiot. So fate could re-unite you and Leatha, and the brothers."

I sat back dumbstruck.
Could that really be true?

His text comes later that night.

Aaron: Meet me at the park.

Thea: I can't. I have to stay in tonight, but I'll see you tomorrow.

Aaron: I want you. I can't wait until tomorrow.

Thea: Have you spoken to your mum?

Aaron: No. I got back late. She's in bed.

Thea: You need to speak to her. I'll see you tomorrow. We need to focus on our siblings,

not ourselves right now.

Aaron: Mercy, please. This could be our last night...

Thea: I'm turning off my phone now. I need to try to sleep ready to face whatever tomorrow brings.

Aaron: Okay. You're right. I'll do the same. I'll speak to my mum in the morning and I'll see you tomorrow. What's the plan? I know you haven't turned off your phone.

Thea: The plan is we never take our eyes off your brother.

Aaron: Okay. Night, Mercy.

Thea: Night, Aaron.

LAST RITES

CHAPTER FIFTEEN

Mercy

In the passenger seat of the car I heard myself calling. "He's there. How are we going to get him to stop?"

The chase went on for another minute, and then the car in front, a black one, rounded the corner. But it didn't make the turn. Instead it hit the wall, rolled, and hurtled over the barrier on the opposite side of the road.

I woke screaming.

Isaac ran into the room.

"Mercy. Mercy. It's okay. You were dreaming."

But it wasn't okay, and as Isaac read my expression he realised.

"You dreamed of the crash again?"

"Yes. But this time it's changed. And he still dies."

The dream stayed with me for hours. A shower didn't wash it away. The day was here—Friday—and now I realised that it didn't matter whether we took Billy's access to his mother's car away because he would be able to find another car and ride the road to destruction anyhow.

"I need to be with him. I'm not going to let him out of my sight."

"How about you ask him over here today? The weather's lovely. Hang around the garden. He could help mow the lawn and stuff. That way I'll be around too."

"Well that just sounds so exciting."

"Exactly. We don't want excitement. We want safety."

I texted Billy and received a reply within a minute.

Billy: sounds good and then later this afternoon we're all meeting down at the coffee shop.

. . .

Thea: Who's we all?

Billy: Everyone's coming. No one's working this afternoon. And Aaron wants to come. He has the day off, apparently he needs to use up some of his leave. He never usually hangs out with his lame little brother. Might have to reduce the PDA's lol.

Thea: Okay, we'll save them for later.

I typed the last bit because later, if all went to plan, Thea would be gone, and in the meantime I could once again give excuses as to why I wasn't kissing him all the time. Because he wanted to. He'd made that perfectly clear, and I'd had to lock lips with him in the garage. Somehow, when I kissed him though it was like I tapped into Leatha's essence and it didn't seem like I was the one kissing him at all. Which was good because my sister wouldn't be all that impressed when I told her I kissed her Earth boyfriend.

And there was my other problem. Because if I did

rescue Leatha from where she was trapped and brought her back to her bed in Andlusan, she would not be happy to stay there. However, that was a problem I refused to give brain space to because at the moment I had a lot larger one than that.

∽

We had tons of fun in the garden when Billy came around. Isaac found some Nerf water guns, and we spent ages firing them at each other. I found some normal Nerf guns in the shed and lined up plant pots on a wall and we spent ages shooting them off in competition with each other. Billy was so competitive I couldn't help but laugh. Isaac made us lunch and then when we were feeling overheated from the sun, we headed inside and I watched Billy and Isaac play a game called Fortnite.

Later that afternoon, we drove to the cafe. Billy asked Isaac if he wanted to hang, telling him that Aaron was coming. It saved us making an excuse for Isaac to appear, so he agreed and we all turned up there together.

Marie and the other girls were there, so I made a beeline for them, asking Billy to get me a coke, seeing as it might be the last one I ever had. Billy's friends, John, Ethan, and Dan were there flicking sugar packets at each other in between staring at their mobile phones. A couple of minutes after our arrival, Aled walked in.

I hadn't seen him since we performed the spell at his house. Without the anxiety of owing money to his supplier, Aled was arrogant and full of swagger. He walked in wearing designer clothing no doubt due to his profits, and slid in at my other side.

"Hey, babe. You want to go somewhere later, just me and you?" He trailed a finger down my face.

"Here's your drink, Thea." Billy was at the table, his shoulders tense and looking like he was about to tear Aled limb from limb.

"Excuse me, Aled. If I could just get past you. I need the ladies." I told him.

He let me out, and his hand brushed not so accidentally across my buttock.

As Billy's fist clenched, I grab his hand, and turning I picked up my drink. "Let's go sit somewhere else, Billy. He's winding you up on purpose."

I knew that Aled continued to watch us closely. Isaac had joined us and then through the door came Aaron. My heart stepped up when those flint eyes met mine and I immediately dropped my gaze to his lips, recalling how they'd met my own that night. I just wanted to spend the day with him—alone—and it killed me that not only could I not do that, but the reality was that I'd probably never see him again.

Unless fate brought you here for him, my mind said. But I couldn't take heed of any thoughts of the future; right now, I had to concentrate on the present. So I carried on moving in the direction of the toilets.

∾

I found Aled waiting for me when I left. He stood in the corridor kicking the wall, bits of old paint and dust fell and gathered on the tiled floor.

"Thea, darlin'. Can you do me a favour?"

I sighed. "Aled. I've come out to spend a nice afternoon with my brother. Can you quit bugging me?"

"Yeah, more like to spend time with Billy Buckley. I get that I'm not good enough for you now you've decided you don't want my goods."

"I was just experimenting. It was a mistake."

He grabbed my arm. "I was, or the drugs were?"

I shook him off. "Both."

"Yeah, well, I don't have any gear on me right now anyway, and that's the thing. I got a bit carried away and spent my money on some new clothes and went and had a bit of a bender, and now, well, my supplier has been round my house and he's not very happy with me. I need a grand like by yesterday, or he says I'm gonna live to regret it."

"Aled, I don't have that kind of money. I have

enough for the cafe, that's it." I shook my handbag towards him. "Check my purse if you don't believe me."

"You fucking liar." He screamed, spittle hitting my face. "I've seen where you live. I've looked through the windows. You have money. You just don't want to share it. You weren't so fucking precious when I was offering to share my stash were you?"

My body was so tense, I felt like my jaw was going to snap. "Aled. My parents own that house, not me. I don't even have a part-time job."

"Forget it." He pushed me and went into the male toilet.

~

"Are you okay?" Aaron came through the door that led from the cafe to the corridor with the toilets. "I told Billy I'd check everything was okay. He's been stuck in the queue to get more drinks for the last ten minutes."

"I'm fine, now he's gone."

"I can follow him into the bathroom and punch him in the nose?"

I shook my head. "It sounds like his drugs supplier is going to take care of him."

For a moment I was lost in thought. No matter that Isaac did the magic spell, Aled had gone down the same path anyway. Thea's fire spell had been withdrawn, but now he was burning his bridges.

"Are you sure you're okay?"

"Yeah. Honestly I'm fine." I looked up into Aaron's steely gaze, seeing the concern there. The—could it be?—Fondness? Affection? My body trembled as the emotion rushed me that this right now could be the last time I saw him alone.

I didn't realise I moved nearer. He grabbed my hair in his hand and quickly pushed his lips to mine.

The kiss was quick but held everything. Then we broke apart knowing Aled would leave the bathroom any second, and we returned to the main cafe.

Our drinks were on the table but there was no Billy.

"Anyone know where my brother's got to?" Aaron asked.

I noted Isaac was not there either and began to panic.

"He said he was going to find you guys; he went to the door." Marie pointed to the glass-filled door that led to the toilets. "Then he turned right back round, grabbed his keys and left, shouting something about traitorous bastards."

"What keys?" Aaron asked.

"The ones on this table. Oh, they were Aled's car keys. Shit."

We were already halfway out of the door, ignoring Marie's panicked stare. Isaac ran towards us from the street.

"Quickly. Get in my car." Aaron shouted unlocking it with his fob.

Isaac jumped in the back. "He went that way." He shouted. "Towards Devil's curve."

∽

"He's there. How are we going to get him to stop?" I spoke the words from my dream as we spotted the Clio RenaultSport Isaac described. The black car I'd seen in my nightmare last night. Only this time it wasn't my sister who had sent him to his death, it was me. If I hadn't moved in closer to Aaron. If we hadn't kissed. If Aled hadn't waited for me to come out of the bathroom. If. If. If.

But now we were on the Devil's curve. The narrow lanes started out quite straight but then became sharp turns and bends running from the town for a few miles, eventually joining a dual carriageway that ran through the countryside and led to the motorways.

We were gaining on him when he must have seen us in his rear-view mirror. The Clio shot forward, the engine screaming.

"What are we going to do? Soon he'll be at the corner where I saw him crash." I yelled.

"I can try a spell." Isaac shouted from the back and he began to mumble an incantation.

Dawn's words came back to me.

'Don't be scared to call upon your powers. Your body will know the way. Just let it guide you'.

I closed my eyes, and I called to the Goddess and the elements, visualised, and I made up the words to a spell and hoped it worked, because we were all out of options.

My highest Goddess
Hear my prayer
He should be here and I
should be there.
Blessed Fate
Hear my plea
Save Billy Buckley
and instead take me.

I found myself behind the wheel of a car I didn't know how to drive. I remembered the brake pedal from my dream and I pressed down on it, pumping and pumping as it refused to work, and then the barrier came towards me and I knew my time here was up.

The next thing I knew, I was standing at the side of a crashed car. A ruined pile of metal looking like an alien among nature. Another car pulled up a safe distance behind, and three men got out. Two of them were shouting at the red-haired one, but he was still, frozen to the spot, and looking directly at me.

My blue gossamer dress blew in the breeze and I had an overwhelming feeling that I wanted to lie down. So I did. I waved to my friend and then I laid down on my back among the flowers and shrubs of the countryside, down the side of the winding lane, and I stared up at a cloudless blue sky. The warmth of the sun filled my body, and then the cold nip began from underneath me, and I was pulled away.

CHAPTER SIXTEEN

Mercy

I came to sitting on the ballroom floor of the Winter Court.

"Next time, if you can tell me you plan to disappear from out of the car that would be helpful." Isaac said with heavy sarcasm, sat at my side.

Staring at him, I shouted the words, "Leatha."

We took off for her room.

As I tore through her door without knocking, Isaac close on my heels, I found my sister awake lying in bed, looking around herself as if she couldn't quite believe she was in her own bedroom.

"You have created quite the drama." Isaac said to her.

"Who are you?" She asked.

Leatha was shaken. She told me she could only now remember a feeling of great unease, of being trapped, but nothing else, nothing visual, and no pain.

Isaac introduced himself and explained how she had become trapped in the planes through her actions.

After we told her what we had had to do to free her, Isaac then told us what had happened after I had crashed the car.

∼

"Remember, time is still here, while it goes on there. Afterwards, Billy couldn't understand how you'd crashed a car and yet no body could be found. Aaron had to take him to one side and explain everything that had happened. His mother had spoken with him earlier that morning, but asked Aaron to explain everything to his younger brother as he'd always taken on a bit of a father-figure role given he was two years older."

Isaac looked from one of us to the other. "He took some convincing that was for sure."

"How come Aaron wasn't fooled by my magic, but Billy was?"

Isaac shrugged his shoulders. "I can only put it

down to the fact Aaron had been in Andlusan for two more years than Billy, four in total, but truly we'll probably never know."

I nodded.

"Anyway, I knew I couldn't leave you much longer, so I took the paper and amethyst and wished for our safe journey's home: mine, yours, and Leatha's. And then we were back here. Myself and Mercy in the room where we performed the spell and left, and you back to your body here."

Leatha rubbed at her head. "This is a lot to take in. I'm so tired. I feel like I've woken from a bad, troubled dream and it's still there."

"We can do a cleansing ritual which will take all that feeling from you." Isaac told her. "Now, I have to tell you, Leatha, that you cannot travel the planes again. You now have a sensitivity to it that means you can get stuck again."

Leatha's face fell. "So I'll never see Billy again?"

Isaac looked at me. "Not necessarily…"

Ramona ran Leatha a bath and Isaac passed her some herbs to place in it before we left the room. Ramona raised an eyebrow at me, but then went on her way, fussing around Leatha as usual.

Isaac returned to my room where Saira brought us breakfast.

"Will I be able to see the painting you are undertaking?" She asked Isaac and I as she poured us a hot beverage.

I sent Isaac a panicked look, but he was too busy eating to notice.

"Er, I-"

Saira placed a hand on my arm, and as I looked at her, she winked.

"You're so annoying." I told her.

"My relatives favoured the old ways. I am glad Leatha is recovering from her *illness*." She said, leaving me in no doubt that her and Ramona had known exactly what was happening.

When she left the room, I turned to Isaac.

"I can't thank you enough, Isaac, for everything you did for me and my sister. I need to speak to her, but I hope that we welcome back the old ways and that they exist among the new. If we found a post to offer you in the royal household, would you accept it?"

"I would have to talk to my betrothed and see if she wanted to be the wife of a royal official. I'm sure she would protest at having to live in the palace and hold a title as a nobleman's wife." He said drily, and then laughed.

I took my hand away from where I had placed it

over my open mouth. "Isaac. I am so sorry. I just presumed you were single with you being so willing to come with me to Earth. I wouldn't have wanted to take you away from family."

"But we've only been gone minutes." He reminded me.

"So we have. Goddess, this is so confusing. I remember that one minute and forget the next." My thoughts go to Aaron and Billy. "What else happened after I left?"

"The car Billy took was Aled's. The brakes had been tampered with. The police arrested Billy. It looks like he'll get a community service order. We think they'll be lenient because it was a drug dealer's car, and they found drugs in it which they linked to Aled. Aled was also arrested. He grassed on his supplier seeing as they'd tried to harm or kill him."

"Goddess. Poor Billy."

"After that, Dawn talked to the boys about what they wanted to do. She'd asked me to wait outside and after a while I joined her. They want to come home, to Andlusan."

I gasped. "Really?"

"Yes. The boys said they'd never felt truly at home in Hallbridge and that they had no ties to the place. All of them want to see Lord Thomas. So I am here on their behalf to petition you and your sister. May they return?"

"You know my answer would be yes. However, I need to talk to Leatha and tell her all that happened between Dawn and my father. Leave it with me this morning and I shall get back to you post haste."

He nodded. "You can send word. I would also like to petition that when the new reign is upon us more modern methods of communication are researched." A smirk followed.

"Yes, I'm not sure I can do without a mobile phone now." I giggled.

"I will go perform the cleansing spell and then I shall take my leave."

I stood and hugged him. "Thank you for everything, Isaac. And should you like to borrow the ballroom for a wedding reception, it would be an honour to host such an event for you."

∽

I bathed for a while and tried to gather my thoughts on recent events. Later when I entered her room, Leatha sat on her chaise looking out of the window.

"In some ways it seems like only a dream." She uttered. "Look at you. I don't think you've been in my room this many times in a year."

"Yes, I have apologies to make. I've been so busy worrying about the reign of Andlusan and its people, I forgot we have to live too."

Her eyes met mine. "I also have to apologise. Because I forgot that while I carry on with my fancies, I leave you to do all the boring stuff. My selfishness means you don't have any fun yourself."

"Well, how about we try to meet in the middle somehow?"

"That would be amazing, Sister. I have a proposal that I would like you to put to Mother's advisors. They would have to ask permission of the other Courts." She then whispered in my ear.

After, I spoke to her of what had happened with our father.

"It was an accident, and it sounds like she has been punished enough." I breathed a sigh of relief that Leatha agreed with me.

"Yes, time passed in both realms for Lord Thomas and Dawn. It was not a simple case of time travel like we did."

"So, let her come back if that's what she wishes."

"I shall ask Isaac to speak to Lord Thomas. You know this means Aaron and Billy shall return?"

Leatha smiled. "What a pity. We shall have to spend time with them again."

CHAPTER SEVENTEEN

Mercy

Our eighteenth birthdays were upon us. Bright blue skies contrasted with the ice on the windows. On the sill I found a single white fluffy feather. "Is that a birthday gift from you, our parents?" I said to the room. "As I trust you are back together now and happy. If this is true, please show Leatha and I more feathers today if you can. Just this once so we can know you are close and agree with what we are doing in Andlusan."

"Talking to yourself is a sign of madness you know, Miss Mercy Elizabeth Northcote." Saira announced as she walked into my chamber.

"I am sure I am destined for future madness." I smiled at her. "To be madly in love with an Aaron

Richard Buckley. Or as he shall now relinquish his mother's maiden name and take his father's surname back, Aaron Richard Mandrake."

Yesterday, Dawn, Aaron, and Billy had returned to Andlusan. Many tears of happiness, and also regret of the years that had passed and been lost, were shed. I had only time for brief words with Aaron, to hope he settled quickly and that I would see him after the coronation. Then he and his family had gone home.

Saira unwrapped my dress from its hanger. A pale blue chiffon, it was covered with a design of snowflakes, and intricate beads and jewels in silver made it sparkle. I would look every bit like the princess I was. And this time my sister had ensured my dress was just as dazzling as her own. For she had petitioned the Courts to ask that we be allowed to rule together. To share the burden as the twins we were so that we could also share the time to have fun and live life. The other Courts had unanimously accepted our petition.

∽

And so it was that myself and Leatha attended our

coronation and were pronounced Queen Leatha and Queen Mercy of the Winter Court of Andlusan. The celebrations went on through the night, all villagers invited for a day and an evening of merriment. It was also announced that the old ways would once again be welcomed here.

I stood at the side of my sister and looked out among the revellers. "We did it, Leatha. Now, don't forget you agreed to share the paperwork."

We looked to our front as Aaron and Billy approached us.

"And don't forget, you agreed to share the fun."

As the men stood by our sides, out of nowhere white feathers appeared to fall from the sky, but yet nothing gathered at our feet.

"You are seeing this too, aren't you?" My sister looked at me with a furrowed brow.

"It is a sign I asked for from our parents, that they are happy together and happy with our plans for Andlusan."

Leatha looked to the skies. "We love you and will make you proud."

"I have no idea what you women are wittering on about, but would you care to dance, Queen Mercy?" A certain handsome man asked me.

"I thought you'd never ask." I replied.

I stole Aaron away to the ballroom on the unused East Wing. After I uttered some words, the piano began to play on its own.

"Get you." He smirked. "Learning your craft so quickly."

"It is coming to me like breathing." I told him.

"I know how that feels." He said, turning to the room and muttering an incantation that lit every candle in the room and dimmed the lights.

"You were unbound." I stated.

"Yes, though that's one of the only things I know how to do. I thought it might come in handy while I wooed a Queen."

"I shall look forward to more." I told him.

He placed a hand in his jacket pocket and brought out a box that belonged to a store from Earth. He opened it to reveal a silver charm bracelet.

"Happy birthday." He whispered. "I bought it before we travelled."

As he fixed it on my hand, I took note of the charms hanging from it: snowflakes, icicles, and beads of a pale blue and white.

"It's beautiful." I told him.

"Like its new owner." He held me close and we began to dance together.

"So, I know you shall be busy with matters of the Court, but do you have time in your life to date a villager? I have no high status here, but I do have a heart bursting to love."

"Oh, Aaron. Did you not know that you are to become staff of the royal court? Lord Aaron, you shall manage the stores and bring them up to date with modern times, and Lord William shall work with our historians. You will need to spend lots of time over at the palace."

"Such a hardship." He said, as he pulled me close and whispered in my ear, making goosebumps feather down my skin.

"It's not the only thing that's hard." Aaron whispered, and I jolted back, smacking him in the arm, and seeing his smirk.

"Aaron Richard! Have you brought your uncouth Hallbridge manners home with you?"

He pulled me close to him again, still laughing.

"That was my first time you know, under the tree?" I said cautiously as I looked up at him, our bodies moving together in time to the music. "And I don't know how real it was given I was a kind of ghost girl. So, I think you might have to do it all over again. My room is about five minutes walk from here and everyone else is so distracted with the celebrations..."

"Then let's make it real. Give you no doubt whatsoever that you are mine." He trailed his hands down my face.

"One day, Queen Mercy, the celebrations will be for the both of us. I am sure of that."

"I hope so." I told him. For I was back in Andlusan, but he felt like home.

THE END

The sisters' rule is threatened by an unknown assailant in FIRST RULES, the second part of this duet.
Out June 8th 2019

First Rules

FIRST RULES

CHAPTER ONE

Leatha

I remembered being in the car as it turned the corner and Billy pumping the brakes.
The brakes that no longer worked.
Then nothing, except a plea to my sister for help before it all went black...

My eyes opened, and I found myself staring at my bedroom ceiling. I was back home in Andlusan in the Winter Court. My heart thudded in my chest as a heavy feeling of foreboding invaded my body, feeling like it was choking me from the inside out. A deep unease that something wasn't quite right.

Then my door burst open and my sister came

running in. A man I'd never seen before hurried behind her. His hair was strawberry blonde and his eyes a vivid green. They carried an expression of concern that I didn't comprehend, given I'd never seen him before in my life. I pulled my covers up around my shoulders. I felt like I needed to shake my body, as if by doing so I could lose this feeling of darkness. It was as if a cloak of something 'other' lay around me, something I found difficult to describe, but needed to be free from.

"Leatha. You're here. Thank the Goddess." My sister began to cry, flinging her arms around me.

"What happened? I travelled to earth and there was a crash and then I remember nothing. Just a feeling of being trapped, uneasy. Please tell me what's been going on." My words tumbled out with haste and a panic of wanting to know what had happened to me and what had happened to Billy.

"You have created quite the drama." The strange gentleman told me, his eyes assessing me as he stood there in his formal suit. I assumed he was a physician, as the gaze that looked me over had no interest in it other than that of someone checking for a pulse.

"Who are you?"

He bowed before me. "My name is Isaac Stafford. I helped your sister with bringing you back from where you were trapped between the planes; and also with saving the life of Billy Buckley. Things have been quite eventful, and I'm mindful of the fact not to overburden you with too much information until you have been assessed by your physician."

Billy was alive! Thank the Goddess. Questions assaulted my brain, causing a pain at my temple.

I rubbed at my head. "This is a lot to take in. I'm so tired. I feel like I've woken from a bad, troubled dream and it's still there."

"We can do a cleansing ritual which will take all of that feeling from you." Isaac reassured me. I breathed a sigh of relief. I didn't know this man's background, but if he knew a cleansing ritual and had helped with my rescue, I could hazard a guess that he knew something of magick. And a cleansing ritual was exactly what I needed to take away this feeling of a shadow around my soul. Isaac met my gaze, a solemn look in his own. "Now, I have to tell you, Leatha, that you cannot travel the planes again. You now have a sensitivity to it that means you can get stuck again."

No travelling? No escape from Andlusan? No... Billy?

My face fell. "So I'll never see Billy again?" My travels had taken me to a different life on earth and had shown me love. Was I never to see any of that, or him again?

Isaac looked at me. "Not necessarily..." He looked at Mercy. "However, I wish to get this cleansing ritual performed immediately so that you may feel better and recover. I shall leave it to your sister to discuss with you the future of you and the Buckley brothers."

The Buckley brothers? My eyes found my sister's, and she blushed.

Well, it would appear a lot had happened while I had been trapped in the planes.

"I will leave you to bathe and will return later to update you on everything that happened while you were... away." My sister left the room and after Isaac had explained the ritual so did he.

Ramona, my lady-in-waiting, ran me a bath and placed the herbs in it that Isaac had given us. She fussed around me, helping me out of my nightgown.

"I shall burn this. Just in case." She told me. I felt a crease form at my brow. "Saira and I are aware of the old ways. Your sister told us nothing; but you can trust me, just as you always have. It is better that we burn that in which you travelled. That we cleanse you of everything."

I nodded.

"Thank you, Ramona."

She tilted her head towards my now steaming bath. "Let us get you into the tub and perform the ritual."

My body welcomed the warmth as I sunk beneath

the water. Flower petals and leaves floated across the top of the water and there was a smell of lavender, rosemary, and other fragrances I couldn't bring to mind.

"There are some words for you to speak, Leatha."

In public, Ramona addressed me as 'Your Highness' but within my private chambers we addressed each other by our given names. I considered Ramona a friend, something not easily found as a royal in the Winter Court.

She passed me the paper and I read it over before speaking the words aloud.

"I call to the Goddess
 To bless this water
 To purify the body
 Of her blessed daughter.
 To remove the shadows of what passed before
 To calm, care, protect, and restore."

The water glowed a luminescent pale blue, and it slowly began to swirl around. Rivulets of water trailed up my neck, and over the parts of me that weren't already covered by the bathwater. Though Ramona's lips parted slightly as it happened, she showed no fear of what she witnessed before her, and

I wondered what indeed, she knew of the ways of old.

The water receded from my body, the light dulled, and I knew the spell had been performed by the fact my body felt tired but lighter. The darkness was gone. I breathed a huge sigh of relief and then my stomach gurgled loudly, breaking the tension I hadn't realised had been there in the room, as Ramona and I giggled together.

"Let's get you out of there and into some clean clothes and then I'll call the cook to fix you some dinner, lest there be reports of the sound of an earthquake in the palace." Ramona laughed.

After I'd eaten, Ramona left me to tend to other tasks around the palace. I sat on my chaise and stared out of the window that looked out over the front of the palace. The frost glistened on the ornate stone staircase leading up to the main entrance; the dragon statues at either side ironic given dragons were known for breathing fire and the Winter Court was known for its coldness.

A knock came to the door and Mercy walked in, taking a seat at the side of me.

"In some ways it seems like only a dream." I told

her. Then I smiled wryly. "Look at you. I don't think you've been in my room this many times in a year."

Mercy looked at the floor, a blush coming to her cheeks, then she looked back up, directly into my eyes. "Yes, I have apologies to make. I've been so busy worrying about the reign of Andlusan and its people, I forgot we have to live too."

"Well, I also have to apologise." I told her. "Because I forgot that while I carry on with my fancies, I leave you to do all the boring stuff. My selfishness means you don't have any fun yourself."

We agreed to meet in the middle and to get our advisors to approach the other courts and see if we might share our rule, given we were twins; rather than my having to take on the Kingdom despite being born only minutes before. Then Mercy told me about how Billy's mother was Lord Mandrake's wife, and about how she'd accidentally killed our father and been banished from the court by our mother.

I called Ramona to make us some sweet tea while I pondered everything I'd just been told. After my drink, I made my decision. "It was an accident, and it sounds like she has been punished enough."

Mercy looked relieved. "Yes, time passed in both realms for Lord Thomas and Dawn. It was not a simple case of time travel like we did."

"So, let her come back if that's what she wishes." *And that way I would see Billy again.*

"I shall ask Isaac to speak to Lord Thomas. You know this means Aaron and Billy shall return?"

I smiled. "What a pity. We shall have to spend time with them again."

Mercy broke into a huge grin.

"Now, Sister, I want to know everything about your visit to Earth and how you managed to romance the very moody Aaron Buckley. I think that is more of a feat than your time travel."

She elbowed me in the arm. "Hush with you. Aaron is wonderful. I am so happy that they will be able to return to their home and be re-united with their father."

"Yes, well, just remember this is not a fairy tale we're in and this is all the happy ever after. Dawn and Lord Thomas have been separated for a long time, and Billy and Aaron barely know him. Now, what are we going to do about the fact that we now know we are the next generation of a family of witches? We not only have our coronation to discuss, but whether we herald a return of the use of white magick, herb lore, healers, etc. It has been years since our mother banned the use of magick in the Kingdom.

Mercy sighed and rubbed at her temples. "There is so much to consider. But for now, you need to rest and reflect on everything that has happened recently. I will leave you to recuperate and tomorrow I will arrange for us to hold a meeting with the court officials so that we may discuss our coronation and any other pertinent issues such as how to rescind the ban."

"Still so serious, Sister. What else shall we do, in order to have some fun?"

My sister smiled. "We shall discuss what we are going to do to welcome back Aaron and Billy. I'm sure there will be some fun in that." Then she winked at me, and I realised that recent events had changed us both.

After an evening meal of a hearty stew, Ramona helped me into my nightgown. I bade her goodnight and returned to my chaise to stare out of my window at the clear and cloudless night sky patterned with a myriad of silver stars. I was exhausted. My mind felt like it had been turned inside out and back to front, and before long I felt my eyes closing. I knew I should move to my bed, but I didn't have the strength.

I was somewhere but nowhere at the same time. I could see nothing and couldn't move. It was like I was suspended in midair and held by invisible threads. I felt a mental prodding at my temples like someone was trying to read my mind.

"You shouldn't be here, girl. This is what happens when you mess with that you don't know." The voice travelled around me, not coming from any definite source.

"Who are you? Where am I?" I called out.

"You are trapped, like a fly in a spiderweb. That's what you are." The voice replied and a hollow laugh followed. "It's been a while since I had company. Those of us in the planes like to share our prizes. You are mine."

That probing sensation came to my mind again, making me wince. "Stop doing that."

"Or you'll do what?" The voice mocked. "You are in no position to bargain with me here, child. You'd do well to remember that."

Then a feeling came across me like ants crawling down my skin, and thoughts invaded my mind of bodies reduced to dust, burned from the top down, and I screamed into the abyss.

"Leatha. *Leatha.*"

I woke panicking, and clutched at my maid. "What was that? What was it?" I yelled at her.

"Leatha, you were having a bad dream. You're on

your seat, look. You must have fallen asleep there."

I glanced around and sure enough I was on the chaise near the window. Vaguely, I remembered my eyes closing as I'd looked at the stars.

I rubbed at my eyes. "It seemed so real. There was something familiar about it all."

Ramona passed me a tumbler of water. "That's how all dreams are when you've just awoken from them. In a few minutes it will begin to fade and then you'll be able to get back to sleep. Now let's get you into your proper bed."

She'd have only fussed further, so I let her lead me to my own bed and I crawled inside the covers. Once I'd convinced her I was all right and ready to try to sleep again, she went, insisting I call for her whatever the hour if needed.

But sleep wouldn't come because every time I closed my eyes I remembered the nightmare.

And despite the fact I'd taken the cleansing bath and spoken the words to clear me of anything I picked up on travel, I couldn't shake off the feeling that what I'd dreamed was a flashback of the time I was lost; the time I couldn't remember.

Eventually exhaustion won out once more, my last thoughts that I would research 'the planes' the first chance I got.

There were thankfully no more dreams that night.

CHAPTER TWO

Leatha

With our coronation in two day's time, there was no more time for me to wallow in my room. Despite how tired I was, Mercy and I were to go to the council chambers situated within the main part of the palace, where we would meet our council and advisors and discuss business.

I decided I'd be prompt and knocked on Mercy's door. I needed to show willing with dealing with palace affairs; something that bored me rigid.

Mercy's maid Saira opened the door to her chambers and beckoned me inside. "She won't be a moment, Your Highness."

We walked down the vast corridor together, before

descending the stairs and making our way to the huge room. "How did you sleep?" Mercy asked me.

"Like the dead." I told her. I decided not to mention my nightmare. She would only fuss, and to be honest there were enough things to deal with in our immediate future.

"I'm not surprised. Me too. I still can't believe I travelled to Earth." She whispered. "I miss jeans and t-shirts already. Having to walk around in gowns all day is restrictive and bothersome."

"That's another thing we can change." I said, finally finding some enthusiasm for something. "We can keep our fancy attire for ceremonies and royal visits, but perhaps we can introduce softer clothes for our day-to-day?"

"There is much I'd like to change after what I saw on Earth and we shall, but we'll have to do it gradually or the villagers will think we have been brainwashed." Mercy giggled.

We reached the large wooden doors, and I rattled the knocker before entering. A large wooden table surrounded by eight chairs was placed in the centre of the room and all present stood and bowed as we walked inside.

"Your Highnesses." said our Uncle River, our mother's younger brother, on behalf of the council.

The council consisted of River, the lead councillor;

Tredby, the treasurer; two lawyers, and two emissaries whose job it was to travel around on our behalf.

Mercy and I nodded our heads at everyone and took our places around the table.

River took the position of Chair. He began to speak while maids poured tea and provided trays of freshly baked goods.

"So the first point of order. Everything is set for the coronation with-"

I raised a hand to interrupt him. "I'm sorry, Uncle River. We have some urgent business that we would like to put forward."

"Okay..." He looked from myself to Mercy.

"We would like to propose that as twins, born so close, we both rule. Two Queens of Andlusan. I would like for Jed and Alun to travel to the other courts to gain their permission to the change and obviously this would have to be immediate given the date of the coronation."

Mercy added her voice to mine. "We all know I have dealt more with the official paperwork of late. My sister and I have had deep discussions and agree that we should share the rule, the paperwork, the throne, equally between us."

"It is not right that I rule just because my mother birthed me first." I added.

"But that is the way it has always been." Tredby

said. "The first rules. It has been this way for thousands of years. Are you sure this is not because you don't feel capable of ruling alone?"

"I wholeheartedly agree with your joint rule." River clapped his hands, interrupting Tredby. "You were born together. You should rule together. As soon as we are finished here we will set the wheels in motion. Royal life will be much easier if we have two Queens. It means we can do much more business."

"No. It means both of us might get a break from royal duty now and again." I told him. He just smirked.

"I will call the team helping arrange the coronation and make the small changes needed to the ceremony."

"But we don't have the other courts' agreement yet." Mercy said.

"I'm sure it's just a formality." River told us. "They would not wish to turn down a simple request from the Winter Court. We are not one to make an enemy of."

It was true. Our soldiers were cold, brutal, and feared.

River went through the rest of his agenda. "Okay so any other business?"

I explained about Dawn, Billy, and Aaron.

"Ah, yes. That was an unfortunate matter." River said. "The council have no opinion on this, you are about to be Queen, or Queens." He looked at my sister and back to me. "Your decision on whether or not to let them return will be seconded by us all."

"Then it shall be." I confirmed.

"And how will these persons travel from Earth to Andlusan?" Tredby said. His face was etched with lines of tension. The man was old; he must have been in his late-sixties. I felt it was time for him to retire and leave someone new with fresh ideas in his place, but it was something to deal with at a later time.

"I know someone who can perform a spell to get them here."

"Those in your mother's inner circle knew of how and why Dawn Mandrake was banished from Andlusan. So how will you announce this to the village? Will you say she was kept prisoner and her sons raised in secret? Or will this come with the blatant use of magick?"

"It is our intention to remove the ban on the practice of white magick and herald a return to the old ways."

"And you know a lot about magick, yes?"

This old fool was beginning to infuriate me.

"I know Mercy and I are descended from witches and like with anything new, we shall learn of our heritage and of how to embrace it. The craft is not something to fear. It can be used for good, for healing."

"How quickly you forget it killed your father."

"That was an accident and Dawn Mandrake has suffered enough for it." I said curtly. "I would ask that you remember your place here as treasurer and keep your opinions to that of the courts finances, Mr. Ollerton."

Tredby bowed his head. "My apologies, Your Highness. My concerns are just of what side effects could occur from this. You must remember I have been around the palace for a long time."

"Let's move this along and end the meeting." River said, looking pointedly at me with an expression that said, 'shut up'. "We need to get this change to the coronation finalised and right now, that's where people's focus should be. Tomorrow we shall convene again at the same time, where hopefully our emissaries will have returned with good news, and we shall bring back the Mandrake family. Do you have someone in mind to perform this ceremony?" He looked from me to Mercy.

"Yes, our dear friend Isaac Stafford will help with this." Mercy announced. "And if anyone is not keen on the use of magick," she looked at Tredby, "they can be excused. In fact, it is probably better that it should just be myself, Isaac, Lord Mandrake, and my sister."

"I shall be there too to ensure the safety of you both as I promised my sister I would." Our uncle said. "However, yes, I do not feel any other council members need to be present for this. Right. I call the meeting closed." He closed the book he wrote in and I imagined him instead holding an iPad and I sniggered.

"Something amusing, Miss Aleatha Rose Northcote?" River sat back in his chair and folded his arms over his chest.

"No, Uncle." I bit my bottom lip to stop it from curving up.

Mercy tugged at my arm and we nodded to the council and then left.

"So what are we doing today, sister?" Mercy asked.

I looked at her, my eyes wide.

"Are you not staying in your chambers dealing with court issues?"

She shook her head and winked. "Nope. You said we were to have fun. Do you know we don't use the East Wing enough? It has a beautiful ballroom. I think we should go explore and see what we could use the wing for. Maybe a series of rooms where the focus is on fun and spending time together? With large screen televisions and computers. We might have to magic a WiFi connection."

"Were you possessed while you travelled to earth? Where is my sister and what have you done with her?" I was startled at the change in her and found it hard to believe it was because of the surly Aaron Buckley. All I'd ever really got from him was derision and a sneer.

"Do you think my maidenhood is still actually

intact here in Andlusan though I lost it on Earth?" She said sweetly before laughing at my dropped jaw, a wicked glint in her eyes.

"Goddess, what have I started with my travels?" I did a mock faint. Then laughing we ran down to the East wing.

We were so busy having fun that my nightmare faded away into the background, dismissed as any other. After my evening meal, I gathered a few of my books on magick. Isaac had called in during the afternoon and had agreed to teach us the old ways properly. He'd given us some homework about simple things like reading up on the history of magick, and how to do protection spells, wards, and simple healing, along with how to call to the elements. We were quick to learn, and he said the magick was strong within us. Although we'd both done greater magick than he was teaching us, he warned us it was important we started at the beginning and learned wisely and with patience. Mercy had guffawed at that and asked if he'd actually met me.

I sat within my piles of pillows, all tucked up, and began reading through the first book. After an hour, I became bored of reading the basics and started to browse through later chapters. I found one called the

Dark Arts, one word from the chapter standing out —*trapped*.

A shiver ran up my spine as I remembered the nightmare in full as if I'd just experienced it.

I began to read.

Protection spells should always be used, and for the most part are efficient in keeping you safe. However, there are malevolent spirits within the planes looking for an opportunity to escape their bindings. You may hear of possessions, or the worshipping of devils. All of this is explained within this chapter. We call these the Dark Arts. For where most witches and wizards practice good magick, there are those who would attempt to use it for ill. Those persons run the risk of possession or being lost, trapped between planes, in what is termed 'the void'.

I felt uneasy. I had been trapped within the planes, and at the time of the crash and my opening the portal to try to get back to Andlusan, I had not had a spell of protection. However, Isaac had helped me perform the cleansing rite so I should be safe, shouldn't I? The feeling of unease had left me since then. I read on looking for anything that mentioned protection.

· · ·

While protective spells are largely efficient, those working the craft need to remember and bear in mind that there are dark entities out there that could be stronger than they are, for whom the spells have little or no effect.

I closed the book. Reading it was just creating madness in myself. All I'd had was a simple nightmare. What I needed to do now was to concentrate on the fact that after my night's sleep there would be a brand new day where my boyfriend would arrive in Andlusan. I called Ramona to help me tidy and prepare for bed and I asked for a sleeping draught. Although a crease came to her forehead, Ramona brought me the brew, and left. I murmured some words of protection, drank the brew and slept.

CHAPTER THREE

Mercy

Thank the Goddess my sister was returned and safe. We had some very busy days ahead of us and I was mindful that I would need to keep a close eye on my sister. She had been trapped between the planes and yet there was no time for recuperation, not with the coronation upon us and the return of the Buckley family. I wondered if they would change their names back to their father's and become Mandrakes?

Isaac had told us that Lord Thomas had cried when he'd heard his wife and sons were to return to Andlusan. The man had cared for us for years and we thought on him like another uncle.

I still had my reservations though about my sister, and her residing in Andlusan, settling in to life as a

Queen with its restrictions. She had a restlessness to her soul, she always had. I hoped that the return of Billy and the many changes that would come to Andlusan would be enough to calm that restlessness within her.

Because otherwise I did not know what we could do to help her.

CHAPTER FOUR

Leatha

It took me time to come around, the lasting effects of the sleeping draught in my system making me yawn uncontrollably.

"Shall I leave you to have some more sleep?" Ramona asked. She was not used to coming to my chambers early; I usually rose late. However, it was a time of fresh starts and new routines, and the tingling sensations in my belly alerted me that sleep was no longer an option. Soon I would see Billy Buckley again. It was just I had to endure another council meeting first.

I was pleasantly surprised to find that instead our uncle met us alone and told us that there had been no objections to our joint rule. In fact, the other courts had welcomed it, thinking it was only fair on a twin birth. The rest of the council were off working and helping with the final preparations for the coronation. Tomorrow we would be crowned. I had far more enthusiasm for seeing Billy again but I kept that to myself.

River ran through the order of the coronation and the day's events. When he was convinced we knew what we should be doing, he ended the meeting.

"So, now for the reuniting of a family. What arrangements have you made?"

We took River with us to the ballroom on the East Wing. "So this is where you've been escaping to." He said looking around. "Such a beautiful room. It should hear music and see dance once more."

"I would rather we stuck to holding our celebrations in the main part of the palace. I like the idea of keeping this area for ourselves. Mercy and I are thinking about transforming the wing into a modern palace. We have such things to show you uncle from Earth that you would believe we were already heavily involved in magick."

"Just remember that we can't be travelling back and forth to Earth. So you must understand that you can't move Andlusan into a time of these phones and computers without engaging with the black market, and I wouldn't recommend that."

"Oh there must be another way. But there is plenty of time to look into such things. For now let us get our boyfriends back."

"Oh Goddess. I hadn't thought about the implications of this. Young love. When I agreed to be your guardian, your mother had just spoken of arranged marriages between the courts, alliances. What have I landed myself with? I shall have grey hair before the week is out. Am I supposed to vet these people? I can't very well do background checks when they've not lived here. Perhaps I should just show them the palace dungeons and warn them that's where they will spend their days if they step out of line?"

Mercy slipped her arm through his. "Perhaps we shall just concentrate on getting them back here and reunited with their father. I have a feeling that they, and we, shall be too busy for romance for the next couple of days at least."

I wondered how the family would take to being in Andlusan after having all the spoils of Earth available to them. I imagined they would feel like they'd fallen down a rabbit hole. It made me realise that the days ahead weren't necessarily going to be the fun times I'd been imagining.

Saira knocked on the door of the ballroom. Behind her stood Isaac and a trembling Lord Thomas.

Mercy jumped up. "Lord Thomas. Is everything all right?"

"He is fine." Isaac reassured her. "Just extremely nervous about his family travelling the planes."

"Then let's get this performed forthwith." I said.

Isaac had been travelling between here and Earth in order to prepare the family for their travel, but he had warned us that after they were here, he would travel no more. We thanked him, knowing we could ask no more of him. Travel could be dangerous, I was testament to that, and Isaac had a fiancee here in Andlusan.

Isaac cleansed the room, throwing salt around at the corners. Once again, I watched my uncle, bemused at his reaction. He'd obviously not dealt in the craft when it had been around Andlusan before. Eventually, satisfied, Isaac called us all to arrange our chairs in a wide circle. Drawing a pentagram on a large piece of paper, Isaac blew burning sage leaves across it before placing it in the centre of the circle.

"I need everyone to concentrate on my words." He commanded.

"Goddess, we give thanks for all your blessings and ask that the journey to be undertaken by Dawn, Aaron, and Billy be protected by yourself and the angels."

He stood and placed an amethyst stone in the centre of the pentagram, before returning to his chair.

"My guides, hear these words and keep from harm,
Dawn, Aaron, and William. Please send them this charm.
May they pass through the planes
Clear from all strife
Please hold them in your blessed arms,
On the travel to their new life."

Dawn

Time still passed on earth while we waited to return to Andlusan. Except we stayed home. We rang in sick to work. We cancelled plans with friends. We waited. And then I felt a warmth at my neck and found a pendant there with a glowing amethyst stone.

"Boys, it's time." I yelled upstairs.

Feet thundered down, and I smiled. Usually I'd

have told them they sounded like a herd of elephants and to take their time so as not to break their necks, but this time I took a seat at the kitchen table and followed the instructions given to me by Isaac. My body welcomed the use of magick once more. It felt like home, because it was. My magick and Andlusan calling to me.

Our makeshift altar was blessed. I looked at my sons in turn.

"Last chance to change your mind."

"Nope. I want to go home." said Billy.

"Say the spell, Mother." Aaron added.

"Okay. Here we go." I took a deep calming breath.

"Send us in flight, our blessed friends.
 Accompany us to our destinations end.
 With our feet on the earth; with the heat of fire.
 Please assist us on travel and ensure we don't tire.
 With the breath of air and the cleanse of water,
 We ask that you protect your daughter,
 And your sons,
 Please grant us safe passage until our journey is done."

The candle in the centre of the table set alight, burning

brightly. Then a sharp gust of air rattled the windows and blew out the candle and my children disappeared before my eyes.

Leatha

The next I knew there were three people standing in the middle of our circle of chairs. They were clutched on tightly to each other. Then slowly they broke apart, looking at their new surroundings.

"Please stay there just a moment while I complete the spell." Isaac stated as Lord Thomas rose from his chair. "Goddess, we thank you for the safe journey of your children. Blessed be."

We all repeated 'blessed be' and Isaac closed down the spell, thanking the elements. Then Lord Thomas burst forth and there were hugs, smiles, and tears as an estranged family reunited.

"We will leave you in here to enjoy some privacy. We will be in the sitting room next door when you are ready to receive some refreshment after your journey, and then we shall ensure you are escorted home-in cover of darkness for now-so that you may recover from the journey." River said to the family.

Lord Thomas nodded, while Dawn looked at Isaac from her place within her husband's strong embrace. "Thank you for everything you have done for us. Your kindness shall not be forgotten." Lord Thomas appeared twice the thin man he'd been before and I realised just how much losing his family had affected him. He had always cared for us greatly, but there had always been a weariness to him, a frailty, and now I knew why.

We retired to the sitting room next door. The room smelled fresh, the windows open, and I raised a brow at my uncle.

"I may have arranged for this room to have been cleaned yesterday. Some of us have to think about what might be needed around here."

I walked over and hugged him. "And that's why we keep you around. This room is stunning. It is such a pity so many parts of the palace are unused."

"Well, we shall have to add it to our forthcoming plans for after your coronation. A re-organisation of the palace and its wings. I trust Mercy will keep your ideas in check."

"Actually, I think you're going to find a more serious Leatha and a more frivolous Mercy in the future." I shot back.

"Isaac. Do you have a protection spell against wayward nieces? I fear for my heart." River jested, though I'm sure there was a small element of seriousness to his request. With boyfriends and the re-introduction of magick, our uncle had more than our new rule to become accustomed to.

Time passed and eventually the family joined us in the room. Dawn hugged Mercy and then I; and then her and Lord Thomas stood chatting to Isaac leaving us with Billy and Aaron.

"I guess this is going to take a lot of getting used to?" I said, weirded out by the distance between Billy and I despite our close proximity.

"Yeah." He rubbed his chin. "I feel like I'm dreaming. Look at you in your weird clothes." He pointed at me. "Apparently I have a wardrobe full of new things to wear. It's like I'm in a play, not real life."

"We'll get used to it." Aaron said as his gaze raked over my sister and a smirk curved his lip. "I can see the advantages to being here."

Mercy beamed back at him.

Isaac walked towards us all. "So, of course, with your sister's journey to Earth it rewrote Billy's past. You remember crashing off the road, but Billy remembered thinking you were with Aaron. I've brought back his memories of the time the two of you spent together the first time around, but Billy could end up feeling confused about things with two sets of memories about yours and Mercy's time on earth.

However, the focus should be on all your futures anyway."

Billy gave me a half smile that did not reassure me at all.

River clapped his hands to get everyone's attention. "Okay, so today has been a very interesting day and I'm sure the Mandrakes are exhausted. Tomorrow is the coronation. We shall need to discuss your employment within the palace as I'm sure my nieces will not want you too far away, but for now, I will arrange the transport to take you home. If you'd like to follow me."

I moved forward and smiled at Billy. "I'll see you tomorrow at the coronation."

"You will." He said, and he leaned over hesitantly and placed a kiss on my cheek. Shivers broke out down my spine at the contact. I craved more. When I'd imagined our reunion, this awkwardness had not formed part of my thoughts. In contrast, Aaron whispered something in my sister's ear that made her cheeks heat, then he kissed the back of her hand. Their passion burned through them whereas I was struggling to raise a kindle of flame in Billy.

The family bade us farewell and everyone left until it was just my sister and I alone in the room.

"Can you believe they are actually here?" She clutched at my arm. "Once we have the coronation out of the way, we can spend so much time together. I can't wait to show Aaron around the palace."

I smiled at her and agreed, but I doubted my joy reached my eyes. The Billy who had just arrived in Andlusan was not the Billy I'd known on earth and I wondered if I'd ever see that version again.

CHAPTER FIVE

Leatha

I woke as Ramona entered my room. She opened the drapes revealing bright blue skies. As I rubbed at my eyes, trying to rouse myself from my half-asleep/half-awake state, she sat at the side of my bed beaming at me.

"Happy eighteenth birthday, Leatha. Today you will be Queen! I am so proud of you, Your Highness."

She gave me a parcel wrapped in a printed paper with crowns stamped on it.

I pushed myself up the bed and leaned back against my pillows, beginning to unwrap the gift. "You know I'll be exactly the same, except everyone out there will call me a different title, right? I'll still be a royal pain in the butt for you to deal with?"

She smiled again. "I wouldn't have it any other way. Now while you wake up properly I will go get you some breakfast and then we shall get you dressed in your finest."

Unwrapping the present I found the most beautiful keepsake box. It was wooden, and painted with the sigils I loved. "Thank you, Ramona."

"It's for you to keep your grimoire and other magick books in. Or anything else of course."

"I love it."

Ramona was so excited and it struck me then that she was about to become the Queen's lady-in-waiting. I'd not given it a single thought. Guilt flooded me as I realised just how selfish I'd been.

"Ramona. I never thought about your gown for today. Do you have anything?"

"Oh don't worry about me, Leatha. Today is about you and Mercy. I have a gown I wear for celebrations."

"No. Today you are to become the Queen's lady-in-waiting and you also need to look amazing. I'm just sorry I haven't thought of this before. You are a similar size to me, let's go and look through my closets." I leapt out of bed with a renewed purpose.

Pulling open the closet doors, I searched through until I found a dress of midnight blue with gems that sparkled across it like the night sky. I threw it at her.

"Go and try that on." I indicated to the screen I always dressed behind.

I could see she was about to protest. "Do you want to upset the future Queen?" I placed my hands on my hips.

"You are so very bossy, Princess Leatha Northcote." Ramona said, but she took the dress from my hands and went to slip it on. Obviously she needed the undergarments to go with it, but for now I just wanted to see how it fitted. My friend came out from behind the curtain looking beautiful. Her silver-blonde hair complemented the gems on the dress.

"You look stunning." I told her truthfully.

"I don't feel worthy to be dressed in a gown belonging to a princess. I should wear something of my own."

I shook my head vehemently.

"Things are changing, Ramona. I am going to have your own rooms upgraded and we shall go through my closets and also get the seamstresses to make you some new gowns of your own. I can only apologise that for the last seventeen years of my life I have been too selfish to spoil one of my oldest and dearest friends who just so happens to be my most loyal attendant."

"Leatha. I have a voice of my own. If I had needed anything I would have requested it. I have perfectly nice quarters next door and many lovely gowns. I have hardly been going without."

"But you deserve more and as the lady-in-waiting of the Queen, you shall have a new wardrobe of clothes and all the accessories needed to go with them."

"Have you had a bang to the head? Where is all this coming from?"

I shrugged. "I just feel that I've been so wrapped up in my own selfish thoughts, that I've not considered anyone else. My travelling caused such tragedy. If it weren't for Mercy, I could have died; Billy could have stayed dead. I just want to celebrate life and I just feel so grateful to have so many wonderful people around me." Tears came to my eyes. Ramona was there in a second with a handkerchief.

"It is an emotional day, Leatha. You only recently lost your mother, and now you and Mercy are about to be crowned. Do not punish yourself further about what has happened in the past. Look to the future. You can create change in Andlusan for the better. You will marry and have children. This palace will be so blessed when there are little princes and princesses running around its halls once more. There is no point dwelling on the past. It is done."

"You're right. What would I do without you, my sensible friend?"

"You'd lie in bed all day. That's what you'd do.

Now let me get out of this dress for now and get you ready. Once you are set, I'll get changed myself. I need to speak to Saira now there's a change to my own outfit."

"I realise it's late but if you and Saira need anything else, just contact the seamstresses and get whatever you need."

"Your generosity is as big as your heart. And it is that which will benefit Andlusan the most. Now let's get you prettied up and pretend it's for the coronation when really we know it's to impress a certain new member of the village."

I grinned. "I can't possibly work out what you are insinuating."

The morning passed quickly. Mercy and her lady-in-waiting Saira, moved into my chambers so we could all get ready together. Mercy was dressed in a blue chiffon gown decorated with a design of snowflakes and embellished with intricate beads and jewels that made it sparkle. She wore a garland of blue flowers on her head which would be removed and replaced with a crown. My own dress was more daring than demure. The top of my dress was white with a black lace overlay to the chest and then white taffeta cascaded out in a vast skirt. I'd had my arms hennaed with the sigils of protection and my skirt carried a few black embroidered ones. It would give the court and the villagers a sign that things were indeed about to change. Ramona braided my hair into a thick plait down my back whereas Mercy wore hers long and straight.

My sister had taken out her own midnight blue dress and a seamstress had made quick alterations to the length for Saira who was a little shorter than the rest of us. Our ladies-in-waiting looked amazing with their hair up in buns and a crystal-jewelled flower clip attached to the front of the bun.

A knock came to the door and our uncle came in.

"It is time for me to escort my very beautiful nieces down to the village square where I shall proudly watch them become queens. Eighteen years old and so beautiful. Your mother would have been so proud." His voice broke with emotion and we rushed over to him as fast as our gowns would allow and hugged him. Guards were waiting in the corridor to escort us. Our security was tight and yet they were never obtrusive, like shadow guards. The doors to the palace opened and I gasped. The villagers lined the pathway holding lit candles and cheered as we began to descend the steps ready to climb into the royal carriage.

And then we were on our way.

. . .

The carriage slowly travelled down the main path of the palace, out of the gates, and made it's way up to the village square. A thick white carpet ran from where we alighted, up to the stone stage where villagers were more used to watching plays than coronations. Upon the stage were two large thrones which looked like they were carved from ice when actually it was glass. The ice glistened on the rest of the floor. At the side of our thrones, just a little further away, were two smaller carved wooden seats with ornate arms where our ladies-in-waiting were to sit.

The crowds had followed the carriage and were gathering in front of the stage. Seats were placed at the front for travelling dignitaries, the council, and invited privileged guests and I spotted Billy with his family. He caught my gaze and smiled. I took a deep breath as I stood in front of the carriage and Mercy grabbed my hand. "Come on, Sister. The sooner the ceremony is done, the sooner the partying can start."

We took our seats on the thrones and the cleric of the courts began the official ceremony. Around thirty minutes later we were crowned and platinum crowns festooned with diamonds were placed upon our heads.

"Please be upstanding for Queen Leatha and Queen Mercy." The cleric said. Everyone before us stood. "And now please show your fealty to your rulers." I watched as everyone bowed and curtsied.

Although I'd been used to such things being born a princess, seeing all these people before me, people dependent on us for their safety and wellbeing, disconcerted me. The weight of responsibility weighed down heavily once more, reminding me that my life was not my own and no matter how much partying and celebrating took place that night, I would never be able to truly let go.

But we were already making one change as new rulers.

I stood before my subjects. "Before we go to greet our guests and the celebrations begin, Queen Mercy and I wish to announce that as part of our reign, the ban of white magick is lifted." Gasps and cheers rang out around the crowd. "More information shall be forthcoming officially from the courts."

Mercy took over from me. "So now, we would welcome anyone who has an affinity with the old ways or who simply wishes to join in, to welcome Mr Isaac Stafford who shall now perform a blessing of our coronation."

A nervous looking Isaac took to the stage. I saw that some of the crowd did break away and others looked on with fear, but others began to clap and cheer. It would take time to adjust, but it was just another part of the change of rule. Some would welcome it, some would oppose it, but all would have to accept it.

Isaac called to the elements, and asked that our ruling be blessed and that we be protected by the angels and it was done.

We announced the festivities had started and the evening began with its entertainment and feasts. Mercy and I had to meet with royals from the other courts and anyone else of importance who had travelled to see us and then we began to accept congratulations from our own. A private banquet took place in the palace and it was late evening before we were free to enjoy the remaining hours of the celebrations the villagers were taking part in.

I watched from the outskirts as a couple danced with complete abandon; merry on wine, food, and love, and I envied them. Mercy came and stood at my side.

"We did it, Leatha. Now, don't forget you agreed to share the paperwork."

She said it as a joke, but the truth of it made my bones ache.

Then Billy and Aaron joined us, standing at our sides and the weight of my responsibilities fell away.

Billy took my hand and Aaron Mercy's as we gazed out.

As we stood there white feathers came from nowhere, appearing to fall from the sky. They fell around our feet in a thick carpet.

"You are seeing this too, aren't you?" I could feel my brow furrow as I wondered if I was going crazy.

Mercy smiled. "It is a sign I asked for from our parents, that they are happy together and happy with our plans for Andlusan."

I looked to the sky. "We love you and will make you proud."

"I have no idea what you women are wittering on about, but would you care to dance, Queen Mercy?" Aaron held out a hand.

"I thought you'd never ask." My sister mocked him and they headed off into the crowd of villagers, aware that within the crowd male and female guards looked like other villagers while they kept watch.

"I'm aware that we haven't had much time together, but right now, I would also like to take the hand of my Queen and eat, drink, and be merry." Billy said. "What say you?"

I guffawed at him talking the way the villagers did. "Goddess, yes, please let us have some fun." I followed him to the dance floor where we danced the night away until my feet burned with pain. With a quick kiss to my lips, Billy left me before I took my carriage back to the castle.

Mercy had left with Aaron a while earlier. I did not want to think about what they were doing, but at the same time I envied them. I had been going to give my virginity to Billy on the night of the crash. Now I didn't know what the future held for us. I could only pray to the goddess that my sister was right when she said that everything that had happened had brought the brothers back to us, back to where they belonged.

Ramona helped me prepare for bed; though I would barely recall it, being merry and exhausted. Sleep claimed me in mere seconds.

"I'm here and I'm waiting, watching, for an opportunity to unleash my hell on Andlusan.
Your return to the past will give me my future.
Enjoy your reign, Queen Leatha, while it lasts."

I woke, panting, my hands clutching at my chest. My clock said it was nine minutes past three. I'd been back again in the nothingness, the disembodied voice around me. Something was here? My return to the past gave it its future? While I'd been trapped in the planes what had I done?

I no longer felt like this was merely a dream. Come later in the morning, I would speak to my sister and Isaac. For now, I got out of bed, gathered my grimoire and supplies and spent the next couple of hours performing and repeating protection spells and placing wards.

Afterwards, I dozed on and off, but every time I woke, a feeling of foreboding washed over me.

Then a fast knocking came at the door and Mercy ran in.

"Leatha. You must rise. I heard a commotion and I sent Saira to see what was happening. A villager was left at the gates of the palace. Her eyes were white, Leatha. I called Lord Thomas. He said she had been drained of her soul."

And there it was. Confirmation in my sister's panicked expression and with her words uttered shakily, that I had possibly brought something with me, back from the planes within which I'd been trapped and already it had brought death to Andlusan.

Worst of all, it appeared that despite my protection spells, I was powerless to stop it.

CHAPTER SIX

Leatha

Ramona helped me dress quickly and then I hurried, following my sister to our medical suite in the main palace. We had our own private facilities, but this was there should any of the palace staff become ill.

"So how was she found? Was she collapsed at the gate?"

"No." Mercy's voice softened. "She was hung on one of the gates by her chest."

"Oh Goddess." I cried.

"Thankfully, no-one appears to have seen anything except Uncle River and a security guard. They'd done a last walk around last night to ensure all revelers had left and that's when they saw her.

"Do we know who she is, and who she'd been with?"

"Yes. Her name is Cassie and she lives near Isaac. She was a witch. Isaac is on his way now. She lived alone. Had no family here that anyone knew about."

"Do we know who she was with yesterday?"

"No. Isaac is going to make some enquiries before he arrives, but he must be careful because at the moment we don't want to make a huge fuss over what has occurred. Uncle River is just meeting with the guard from last night to go over what they saw and ask him to keep a close eye on the palace entrance today lest another body be left there."

I gasped. "You think it might happen again?"

She shrugged her shoulders. "It's hard to know what's going to happen. All we know so far is that someone left us a body. Was it a warning? A protest at our announcement of a return to the old ways? A protest at our rule?"

I nodded towards the door where the body was. "Is Lord Thomas in there?"

"Yes. He is waiting for Isaac and erm..."

"And?"

"And a necromancer."

I gasped. "They're going to raise her spirit? Here, in the palace?"

"Keep your voice down." My sister scolded. "What

else are we to do? She is dead and we know not why or how."

"Maybe we could investigate the normal routes before we mess with spirits?"

"There isn't time. We have to do it before the day is passed."

"Mercy, I need to talk to you urgently."

The door to the suite flew open and our uncle dashed through it.

"Right. Allward is positioned along with other guards to watch the gate and perimeter. The others just believe we are raising security for our new rulers. Has Lord Thomas come out yet?"

"No, he is still in there." Mercy answered.

"I will go and see what's happening."

Mercy shook her head. "He said he should not be disturbed and would come out in due course."

"But-"

"No, buts. That's what he said and that's what we will do."

It was the first time since our coronation that Mercy had sounded like the Queen she now was and I saw our uncle's shoulders drop as he acquiesced. "You are right. This is not my area of expertise."

"Nor mine, Uncle River." Mercy shook her head. "The first day of our rule, I expected us to be lying in bed with sore heads, exhausted from dancing; not dealing with a threat to our safety."

"It frustrates me. Threats with swords and pistols I can manage. Sorcery, I cannot."

"You have dealt with the guard who witnessed the incident, put extra security at the gate, and you are here now, Uncle River. We can't ask for any more." I told him.

I needed to tell Mercy about my dreams and fears but I didn't want to do it in front of our uncle, so for now I would have to once again bite my tongue.

For now, we could only wait.

"So I told Aaron last night that he was to become staff of the Royal Court, managing the stores and bringing them up to date, and I may have let slip about Billy being given a post as a historian." Mercy looked at her feet.

"Mercy! That was to be announced in the coming days!" River scolded her. "We haven't even fully agreed it with the council yet!"

She put her hands over her mouth and widened her eyes before dropping her hands to her lap. "I know. I'm so sorry. It was the celebration and drink. It all made me too giddy and I couldn't help myself."

"So, what was his reaction?"

Her blush told me far more than I needed to know. Luckily, our uncle didn't seem to notice it.

"He was very pleased. Especially with it meaning more time spent at the palace."

Our uncle didn't miss that insinuation though.

"He will be here to work, and you will be doing your duties as ruler of The Winter Court. Any time spent at the palace together needs to be outside of working hours, young lady."

Mercy looked at him, schooling her face into an icy expression although her eyes twinkled with mischief. "What I decide shall stand as the Queen."

River laughed. "Nice try, niece, but while you are queen and I will bow to your official role, I am still your uncle. You might be an adult and eighteen now, but I will always be your overprotective uncle and I don't intend to change."

"That's you told." I laughed.

Mercy's expression changed to one of amusement and she looked at River fondly. "Good, we don't want you to change."

"I'm glad. You have both embraced the Wiccan arts. You might turn me into a hound or something."

"Hmmmm, now there's a thought." I joked.

The jovial conversation had given us a welcome reprieve from the events of the morning, but then the door to the room containing Cassie and Lord Thomas opened and Lord Thomas stepped out closing the door behind him.

"Are we able to talk freely?" He looked around.

"Yes, there's just us." River nodded.

Lord Thomas nodded back in acknowledgement, moved forward and took a seat beside us. "It is as I feared. There is nothing at all to suggest a death of natural causes, or for that matter, one of poisoning, or any other murder. The body shows all the signs of a soul draining."

"But why would anyone do such a thing?" Mercy asked.

Lord Thomas shook his head, "I don't know. That's why we need the necromancer."

River's forehead creased. "Is this connected with the return to the old ways? We only announced it yesterday and we're already having to summon a necromancer and raising dead spirits in the palace. I must note my reservations at all of this."

"I understand completely." Lord Thomas said. "But you must understand that magick has been practised since the ban, just behind closed doors. It has never gone away. So I find it hard to believe that this is connected to the lifting of the ban. It could be a protest at the new queens, but again, why after the coronation? Surely a protest would have been better beforehand?"

There was a knock at the outer suite door and River went to open it. Isaac followed him back in.

"Have you learned anything?" Lord Thomas asked him.

"Just that she was seen in the village until early evening and then she told her friend she didn't feel well and was going home. I've told her friend that Cassie was taken ill near the palace and we are treating her. I don't want to announce her passing yet, not until we have more information."

We all agreed.

"So, Tor, the necromancer is outside. Personally, I think the sooner we get to ask questions the better."

And this was it. Once this Tor person spoke to the spirit of the deceased, I might know whether I was connected to the problem or not.

"Then let's begin." I told him.

Tor was a small wisp of a man. He looked around sixteen, but was actually a decade older than that. His hair was short and bright red, his skin pale. Indeed, he dashed around in a way I imagined a mischievous pixie would. We stood at the back of the room containing Cassie. When I'd first walked in, I was pleased to find that Lord Thomas had closed her eyes and she just looked asleep. My heart went out though to the young woman whose life had been ended by another within my kingdom. I would do all I could to avenge her death once I knew what we were dealing with.

Tor moved with haste around Cassie's body, muttering incantations under his breath and moving his hands in the air over the top of her body.

"What is he doing?" I whispered to Isaac.

"Ensuring that the body and anything within it stays on the bed." Isaac responded, making an icy shiver travel down my spine.

When Tor stopped, he nodded his head at us. "It is time. I will ask the spirit to come and indicate when you can ask your questions, but ask wisely because the spirit will not be able to stay for long."

"Lord Thomas. You ask your questions first, in case the spirit tires." I told him.

"Thank you, Queen Leatha." He turned to look at us. "If you could all stay at the back and observe."

Lord Thomas walked to the foot of the bed standing to the right-hand side. Tor was at the left towards the top of the bed. "Okay, Tor. Let's begin."

"Spirit of the deceased. We now call you here to this protected room. We wish you no harm. Cassie Louisa Raglan please wake."

Cassie shot up in the bed, her eyes shining white orbs and I swear I almost died myself of fright. Judging by the fingernails currently half-embedded in my arm, my sister had had a similar reaction. Pale blue light shone around the body showing where the wards were keeping her in place.

"Cassie. Could you tell us how you died?" Lord Thomas asked simply.

The voice that came out was monotone. "I took a drink and felt unwell. I decided to return home. Then voices. Voices told me to let go. To give my body up to-"

Her eyes turned black as night and bloody tears ran down her face. The wards flashed as she leapt from the bed and hit them.

"I will return." She stared right at me. "I grow stronger."

Mercy was being comforted by our uncle, but I stood stock still staring at the figure. I moved closer. I could feel Isaac's hand at my elbow.

"Who are you?" I asked.

"Leatha, you know exactly who I am. You were the one who brought me here."

Cassie laughed, an unholy malevolent screech and then her eyes closed, and her body fell to the floor.

CHAPTER SEVEN

Leatha

"What just happened?" Mercy's voice was an anguished squeak. "What did it mean 'you brought me here'?"

"Let us allow Tor to close the spirit rising and then let Isaac and myself perform some other magick. After, might I suggest we meet in the ballroom on the East Wing and discuss all this further?" Lord Thomas said.

"Yes. That sounds wise." River answered. "Come on, my nieces, we shall make our way there now."

From my uncle's tone it was clear that he wanted answers from me, and he wanted them right now.

"Why didn't you tell us any of this earlier?" River's tone was full of frustration.

"I tried to tell Mercy, but you entered the room."

"Since when did you start keeping secrets from me, Leatha? How am I supposed to protect you, look after you, if you don't tell me when there's a problem?"

I slumped in my seat. "I'm sorry, Uncle River, but I didn't know then that there was one. I was just going to raise my concerns with Mercy and ask her advice, but I did think what I was experiencing was just a bad dream, a flashback to my time trapped, a time I can't recall. It wasn't until Cassie, or the entity within her, said it was me that I knew for sure."

"So now Andlusan has upon it an evil entity and we don't know what it wants." River sighed, rubbing at his temple.

'I'm here and I'm waiting, watching, for an opportunity to unleash my hell on Andlusan'. The words ran through my mind, but I decided I'd wait until Lord Thomas and Isaac were here before I shared this nugget of information.

Thirty minutes later we were joined by the others. "Tor has left and assures us that Cassie's body is now free. What was within has now moved on. I have arranged for the body to be collected and burial shall be arranged in the usual Andlusan way." Lord Thomas said. Our way was to take the ashes of the deceased to the Great Mountain of Ice where they were sprinkled in a lake at the top, so that the deceased could pass back to Winter and its elements.

"Now, I suggest, Queen Leatha, that you tell us everything. As much as you can remember."

So I did. I told them that I still remembered nothing about being trapped within the planes, except that feeling of unease which passed after bathing, but that since then I'd had the dreams of the unknown entity who told me I'd brought it here. That it was watching and waiting to unleash hell on Andlusan.

"So you see, it said my return to the past gave it its future."

Isaac sighed. "It would appear, in my opinion, that whatever was in the planes with you hitched a ride. The problem we have is that we don't know who or what it is." He stroked at his chin. "Lord Thomas and myself are going to need some time to study this and to come up with a plan of action."

"So what do I do?"

Isaac looked at me. "Just rule your kingdom as normal. Until we come back to you."

"You heard the man." Uncle River rose to his feet. "We need to call a council meeting and then tell those boys of Lord Thomas' that they have new roles in the palace. Officially." He side-eyed my sister who looked contrite. "You have learned one important lesson about the rule of a Queen, and that is that whatever happens, life as the ruler goes on."

And with that, we left.

Days passed. I had no more dreams. Billy and Aaron had been given their new roles and were settling in to daily life at the palace. I knew my sister had seen Aaron on a couple of occasions in an evening, but tonight was the first night since our coronation that I was getting to spend any time with Billy. He arrived at my chambers after his working day was finished, looking awkward and not at all like the Billy I knew on Earth.

"Come in." I beckoned him.

He shook his head vehemently. "It is not within royal protocol for me to enter the Queen's chambers."

I huffed exasperated. "Billy. It's just you and me. Please can we just act like we did before?" By before, I meant on Earth, but it wasn't something I could say out loud. The rest of Andlusan thought Dawn and her children had been banished to another court, not another place entirely. Earth was a thing of myth, with gossip and the appearance of items purported to being from there, but with no actual proof as to its existence.

"But it's not just you and me is it, Thea?" Thea was the name I'd used on earth. "Here I'm a newly appointed Lord and you are the Queen. The Queen of Andlusan, of the Winter Court. A woman who shall be expected to marry someone of her own worth. A royal from another court. Here everything is entirely different."

"I don't want it to be. I hate it. Don't you understand that? It's why I travelled to Earth in the first place. This court had become my prison, and now it's doing it again." I felt my jaw clench and my shoulders tighten, while my hands fisted together. "You showed me I could just be me, Thea. Just a simple girl who wanted to live life."

Billy looked defeated as he stood before me. "But that's not who you are here, Queen Leatha."

"Don't call me that!" I yelled. And with a spike of temper, I shut the door of my chambers in his face.

I threw myself onto the bed sobbing, until exhaustion took me over.

"Oh, Queen, does your first rule not go so well?
  It's the start of your descent to hell.
  I will rule and you will fall.
  Then as should be, I'll have it all."

I woke with the voice reverberating in my head.

"Get out. Get out. Get out." I screamed as loud as my lungs would let me.

Ramona rushed in, a panicked expression on her face.

"Leatha, what is it? Another bad dream?"

"Yes." I wept. "I'm so tired, Ramona. I just want to sleep, uninterrupted with no bad dreams."

She hesitated as if debating something within herself.

"My mother practised herb lore and healing spells. I shall make you another tincture."

"The sleeping draught? It was magick?"

She nodded.

I grasped her arm. "Then please, make it me every single night until I find out what is causing these nightmares and stop them."

"Okay, Leatha. Let me go prepare some now." She did, and I drank it greedily, almost burning my tongue in my haste to get a return to peace in my mind.

Then Ramona left me, and I had hours of blessed relief from torment.

CHAPTER EIGHT

Leatha

There was no meeting this morning. The council were busy with their own work. Feeling rested, but bad about what had occurred with Billy, I decided to go and visit Dawn and ask her advice.

The Mandrakes (they had all returned to their original surname on return) lived in royal accommodation within the village. The house was small given that Lord Thomas had lived there alone, and I decided one of the things I would discuss with Dawn was a possible move to a larger property.

In order for me to be left alone, my guards had to be allowed in to inspect the property. Once this was done they stood down outside the building.

"I'm sorry about that." I told Dawn. "It's all very wearisome."

"Are you okay, Thea? You look troubled."

I'd never really had any type of deep conversation with Billy's mother. More she'd fed me and hovered when I was in the house with Billy, but now I needed a mother figure of my own more than ever. I slumped down at her table while she passed me a drink of sweet tea.

"Since I got here, I've barely seen Billy. Yesterday, he came to my room and we had a fight. He wouldn't enter my chambers, because of protocol. Life was so easy on earth, Dawn. I just don't know what to do."

Dawn placed her hand on top of my own. "Life wasn't easy on earth, Thea. You had your problems there too. You're looking at things through rose-tinted spectacles. You were just made Queen. It's bound to be a frustrating time of change and adjustment, and Billy, well, he's just reunited with his father, and has to settle in a place with none of the things he's used to, like his gaming equipment and his mobile phone. You should have seen his face when I suggested he read!" She laughed, and it broke the tension as I laughed back. "Just give him time, sweetheart, and give yourself time too."

I sighed. "You're right. I just want things back to how they were between us."

"I'm sure they'll get there, but I doubt you'll be the same two people. You'll need to find a new way of being together that takes in both your statuses."

"I shall meet him away from the palace and show him around Andlusan. That shall be a start."

Dawn smiled. "That sounds like a good idea. Go and have fun. That's what you two had together before; that's what you need to find again. More fun, less formality, and you'll both find your way back to each other, I'm sure."

I took a deep exhale. "Thank you, Dawn. Or should I say Lady Mandrake?" I winked.

Dawn laughed. "And that also is taking some getting used to."

"Are you beginning to settle in though?"

"Yes." She nodded, but there was something in her eyes, something she wasn't telling me. I wouldn't press, but I hoped whatever it was settled, or she found she could confide in me with time. It was then I realised that I'd come here as her son's girlfriend, as she'd known me on Earth, but Dawn was well aware that here I was also the Queen, and that had placed an unwanted barrier between us, despite our best efforts to avoid it.

"Well, I'd better return to the palace. Thank you for the tea and for the very sensible advice. I shall find your son and apologise for my temper tantrum."

"He'll have forgotten it already, and if he hasn't, blame your menses. That's what I do and then he just pulls a face, places his hands over his ears and tells me to forget it."

I laughed again and then we both jumped as we heard a commotion outside the window. I leapt forward to find a guard holding a woman, a placard at her feet.

Another guard entered the property.

"Please stay back and away from the window until we have dealt with the current situation." He said.

"What's happening?" I queried.

Dawn sighed. "It's a protestor. It's been happening since I returned. They believe I murdered your father and that it wasn't an accident at all. There have been eggs thrown at the windows. It's fine. I'm sure they'll tire of it soon when I show them it doesn't bother me."

Now that unknown element to her expression before was revealed to me.

"Why didn't you tell me?"

"I think you have had enough on your schedule, my *Queen*."

"I will always have time for you, *Lady Mandrake*." I addressed my guard. "Please check that we are safe to travel and then please ask the other guard to stay stationed outside." Dawn opened her mouth to protest. "Lady Mandrake, I shall be discussing with my sister about your safety and future accommodations and I shall be back in touch with you forthwith." I spoke to her like the Queen I was, with a command in my tone that brooked no argument.

She curtsied. "Thank you, Your Majesty."

And then I left to talk to my sister about having the Mandrakes moved to the palace grounds, and to talk to Isaac about an idea I'd had.

Mercy was in complete agreement as I'd known she would be. Let's face it, it brought Aaron nearer, so she wasn't going to protest. Yet, rather than envy her, I was happy for my sister. She'd been living a life of palace officialdom since our mother's passing and I was glad to see her enjoying life. Whereas my life was going in the opposite direction, no fun and palace officialdom. And that's why I wanted to talk to Isaac. It was time to get some fun organised.

"So, Mr Isaac Stafford. When were you planning on making an honest woman out of that girlfriend of yours?"

"As soon as things settle down in Andlusan."

I waved my hand. "That may never happen, my friend. I wondered if perhaps you might like to marry her next week, after officially being made Lord Isaac Stafford? I thought you and your lady may welcome a handfasting ceremony in the woodlands after your official ceremony in the royal chapel. After which, you may choose whether to stay within your current lodgings or take accommodations in the palace grounds where the Mandrakes shall also presently be residing."

His jaw dropped open. "Can you run that past me again? I'm sure you just said I'm being made a Lord, a member of the royal household, and that you will host my wedding."

"That's exactly what I just said. But what say you?"

He grinned. "I most definitely say yes. Let's hope my bride does too on the day!"

Days in the palace got a little more interesting then as I met with Audrey, Isaac's betrothed-a beautiful woman with long blonde hair and cornflower blue eyes-and her family, and we began organising dresses and other wedding paraphernalia. The village got excited at the thought of another celebration, and Aaron and Billy helped their family and Isaac move to two larger properties on the grounds of the palace estate.

Billy seemed lighter and after apologising to one another, we met a few times and I showed him around the palace. Things relaxed between us, although I still only received a peck on the cheek when he left me.

I couldn't help but become a little jealous of Audrey and Isaac, and for that matter my sister and Aaron. They were all so clearly in love.

Wanting to find a little quiet time for myself away from the hustle and bustle of the palace, I informed Ramona that I would be taking a visit to the family mausoleum located at the rear of the palace. It was a pleasant walk through woodland. Of course security had to accompany me, but after a brief search of the building they were happy to let me go inside alone.

The building was huge and housed the stone coffins of our predecessors. I walked down the lit corridor until I reached the tombs of my mother, father, and my grandmother. I sat on a stone bench nearby and took some deep breaths as I relaxed in a place of complete silence. Somewhere I could gather my thoughts.

I'd been very young when I'd lost my father and so regretfully I didn't remember him much. It was a shame we'd never been able to experience family life with a loving father. My mum had loved us but having to rule Andlusan had meant a lot of the time she was busy on palace business. Also, the loss of our father had cost her dearly, scarring her gentle personality and making her hard, cold, and ruthless at times. She'd had to be. Often, I'd spent time with my grandmother. It had been she who had told me that we were descended from witches and who had sparked my interest in investigating more.

"I miss you all." I said out loud. "And I certainly could use your help right now, Grandmother."

As the words left my mouth, a thought occurred to me. Maybe I could talk to her? There was talk of people who could communicate with the dead. If a necromancer could talk to someone by raising their spirit for a few moments, was it possible to communicate with someone who had been passed longer? I sighed. Probably not. They'd said twenty-four hours after death. My grandmother had passed several years ago. However it was something to look into, to prepare ourselves for whatever was coming. Because while there had been nothing since Cassie's death, I didn't think for one moment that it was over.

It was the calm before the storm.

A storm that could destroy my Kingdom, my home, and everyone who lived there.

CHAPTER NINE

Leatha

The day of the wedding and handfasting was upon us. We were leaving it to the families to prepare themselves. Our seamstresses and other staff had been sent to assist and Audrey had a handmaiden now who would take an official post when Audrey became Lady Audrey Stafford.

Mercy and I were ready to take our place in the chapel as ruling Queens.

"Oh my goddess, this day is so exciting. Do you dream of your own wedding day, Leatha?"

I scoffed at her. "Huh, I shouldn't imagine anyone would want to put up with me long enough to marry me."

Mercy tilted her head at me. "Leatha, you are a wonderful person. Look what you've arranged for our friends. That was all you."

"Yes, but did I do it with pure intentions or because I hoped Billy would begin to have fun here and go back to how he was?"

If pity was a gown, Mercy was cloaked in it. "Oh, sister. Their travel here is still so very recent. He will come around."

"He came here with his brother. Aaron doesn't look like he's having any trouble adjusting."

Mercy blushed. "While it's true we are spending lots of time together, he is still finding being with his father something very different. Aaron was used to being the man of the house and now at age twenty he finds he is not. At the same time Lord Thomas wants to be a father, but feels in some ways he cannot, given he hasn't been there for the best part of his son's life."

"See? All this is going on, and I am back to being selfish that Billy is not giving me his undivided attention. I am a fool."

Mercy clutched at my arm and squeezed. "You're not. You're missing him and the relationship you had back on Earth. There's nothing wrong with that. You just need to take a day at a time."

"Because of course I am known for my patience."

We burst into giggles and I linked my arm through hers. "Come, Sister, let us watch our good friends get married."

We sat on two bright white stone thrones either side of the chapel gallery while the chaplain performed the official marriage ceremony before family and friends.

Declared man and wife, we watched as a dapper looking Isaac kissed his beautiful bride. She wore a gown of white silk that flowed simply. It was covered in a silver lace overlay that sparkled in the light. Their smiles were huge, their expressions bursting with happiness as they clung onto one another and stared into each other's eyes.

I looked into the crowd where my eyes met Billy's. For a second, he held my gaze. I saw torment cloud his features and then he looked away. My own smile slipped for a moment, but then I pasted it back on my face and concentrated all of my attention on the bride and groom.

We moved into the woodland near the castle and here one of the villagers Isaac and Audrey had known since their childhood performed the handfasting. I much preferred the simplicity of this service and the being amongst nature. The couple had slipped off their shoes, their feet grounded in the earth. I wanted to take off my own shoes and wiggled one partially off my foot only to receive a sharp elbow from my sister.

The ceremonies complete, we congratulated the new Lord and Lady Stafford and the celebrations began in earnest.

There was a huge feast in the palace and afterwards music and dancing in the main hall. Aaron and Billy walked over to us and Aaron whisked my sister off onto the dance floor.

Billy held out his hand. "Would you care to join me, Thea?"

I beamed at the use of my Earth name, the one he'd always called me. "I would be delighted." I answered.

He took hold of my hand, and despite the warmth of his skin, it caused shivers to run up my spine with his touch. On the dance floor, he pulled me towards him, and we danced to the music, his hand at my lower back. Being in such close proximity was intoxicating. After three dances I gazed up into Billy's eyes and tried to tell him how I felt, that I wanted his lips on mine. He pushed me back gently. "I think we should perhaps get refreshment now? Dancing is thirsty work."

I nodded when he said he would get us a drink, but

as soon as his back was turned away from me, I left through a side door. Passing my sister on my way out I told her that I was going to my room for a short rest as I felt fatigued.

"Is everything okay?" She touched my arm.

"I just need some time out. I'll be fine. Too much dancing!" I joked, but I could see I wasn't convincing my sister.

When I reached my room, I was glad that there was no one around except for the guard stationed outside the door. Once inside, I stripped down to my underwear and put on a robe. My feet were bare against the carpet and although it wasn't the bare earth I'd wanted to walk on, I still welcomed being out of my footwear.

I picked up a romance novel I had sneaked back from one of my visits to Earth, and began to read about true romance; the kind that pulled on your heartstrings and you wished for more than anything. Being with Billy made my stomach fizz and feelings appear in other places, but maybe I had to accept that he was no longer interested and free him to romance someone he felt more at ease with?

A knock came to the door, and the guard came through.

"Lord William is here to see you, Your Highness."

No time like the present. I may as well get this over with.

"Send him in. Thank you."

The guard bowed and moved back to let Billy in while I got out of my bed, wrapping my robe further around me.

Then he was there, and the guard had closed the door.

Billy cleared his throat. "Are you okay? I came back from getting the drinks and your sister said you'd excused yourself. That you were tired?" He said the last sentence as a question.

"Yes, that's right." I nodded and then using my right hand I gestured between the two of us. "I'm tired of this. It's obvious you can't cope with me being Queen, that you can't see me as a woman anymore. So, fine; you're free, Lord Mandrake. Go find someone you consider on your level."

Billy's jaw gritted. "Can't see you as a woman? That's all I can see, Thea." His voice rose as he stalked toward me and I swallowed. "Do you have any idea what it's like, trying to keep myself under control when I'm around you? Trying to respect you as you're now my Queen? I know what we both had planned for the night we crashed. I'd run my fantasies of what might happen over and over." Reaching out, his hand trailed down my cheek.

"I'm trying to do the right thing. What's the protocol for dating a Queen?"

"And that's what I'm saying. You can't see past my title. I am Thea to you. Do you understand me? Thea first and the Queen second. Fuck the protocol. I'm Queen, I can change it if it doesn't suit me."

A smirk came to his mouth, a slight uplift at the corner. "I swear you've more balls than I have."

I couldn't help myself. My eyes fell to his groin.

"Fuck it." He said, sounding so much more like the man I knew. He pulled open my robe and let it fall off my shoulders revealing my thin vest and panties. My nipples pebbled underneath my shirt.

"Fuck me." I whispered uttering the words I'd read in the book.

His breath hitched as he picked me up and threw me onto the bed.

"You sure about this?" He looked down into my eyes.

I nodded back at him. "So very sure."

Then his lips were on mine. No chaste kiss on the cheek, but hard, bruising kisses that made my lips swell. His tongue pushed into my mouth tangling with my own. Then he was on the move. His lips trailed down my neck and he pushed up my vest revealing my breasts and took each into his mouth in turn. I arched towards him. "Dear Goddess."

"It's not the Goddess you answer to or thank now." He whispered. "It's my name you need to scream."

I felt my arousal between my thighs before his mouth moved down and he licked me right *there*. I was almost delirious with pleasure and while I knew from my teachings that it would hurt, I needed this man inside me.

He moved back up, lined himself up at my entrance and pushed gently.

I thought I would tense up, but I didn't. Slowly, he edged in and while I felt a little burn, I also felt pleasure.

"Are you okay?"

"I'm fine, don't stop."

And then he was inside me and he moved gently at first, rocking in and out. My pleasure began to build, the pain went away and our movements became frantic as we rode together, lost in each other's bodies.

Next, I was flying, as my core clenched around him and I saw stars.

We stayed in each other's arms all night. I told Ramona that I didn't require her services. Later we made love again, and it was even better. I couldn't get enough of Billy.

And it all just felt right in that moment. That whatever I faced in the future, I faced with both Billy and my sister by my side. I could see a way forward with my rule. A balance between protocols and village celebrations, along with time to learn my craft. And for the first time I allowed myself to see a future with a consort and a family. My consort looked a lot like Billy. I knew it was early days and stupid, but I'd always been given to fancy and I wasn't going to stop now.

So that night's dreams hit me that much harder.

Isaac and Audrey stood at the altar in the woodland in a scene exactly like the handfasting ceremony. Except as the witch spoke, the ground trembled slightly.

The guests all looked at one another wondering what the tremor had been.

And then it came.

Every leaf, every flower, every blade of grass turned black with disease, death, and decay and the blackness spread like a forest fire travelling up the aisle and putting darkness beneath everyone's feet.

As the witch closed the ceremony and took hold of the rope that had been laid over the couple's hands, the decay spread up the rope, reached her hands and went through her body, turning her skin black. Blood poured from her eyes and spilled from her lips dripping to the ground where it sizzled as it met the earth.

"I will find a worthy host." The words boomed inside my head, as the body of the officiant fell to the ground, her eyes turning white and soulless and I woke up screaming.

CHAPTER TEN

Leatha

"Leatha!"

I woke to find myself being shaken gently.

"You've been dreaming. Be calm. Seriously. It's okay. It's just a dream. I'm here."

Throwing myself into Billy's arms, I sobbed loudly.

"I don't think it is. Billy, I think it's real." I cried. Then I told him about my nightmares and the dead villager.

"Okay. Firstly, we need to know if what you dreamed is the truth. So get dressed and the first thing we'll do is take a walk to the woodland. Once you see it's intact and as beautiful as ever, we'll check on Greta, the officiant, and then I'll get Ramona to run you a hot bath and you are going to relax."

"It's true, I know it." I told him. I felt it inside me. Something deep in my mind, as if someone were whispering the truth.

Billy stroked a hand down my hair in a soothing motion. "Leatha, it's probably all a result of the stress you've been under. Being trapped in the planes, then having to rule. It's bound to take its toll. I'm not saying that there isn't something out there, but the chances are it was on your mind and that's why you've dreamed it so vividly."

I pulled on my clothes quickly.

"The sooner we get to the woodland the better." I wouldn't rest until I'd seen with my own eyes everything was okay, but I was sure I'd not be resting again.

Two guards followed behind us, but I didn't have to go right to where we had stood just yesterday. I could see from the edge of the woods. A black path scorched the earth from where the wedding party had walked, as far as the eye could see.

I fell to my knees.

"Take her back to the palace." Billy told the guards. "I need to check something out." He lifted my chin until I caught his gaze. "Get your sister, tell her what's happened, and sit with her until I get back. I'm going to the village to call on Greta."

FIRST RULES

. . .

I barely remembered the hours that followed. Greta's body was discovered in her home. Her body was completely blackened, apart from the dried crimson that had run from her eyes and her mouth. But it was worse. A field full of cattle next to a series of villagers dwellings had suffered the same fate. Every one of the cows lay dead in the field, their skin blackened, and the same crimson tears decorating their faces. The same white blank stare that shook your own soul. And the villagers screamed of a curse, causing panic to set into Andlusan.

Protestors to the use of magick were at the castle gates, screaming that our rule should end, that we were witches and we had caused this. River sent out his guard and passed off the death of the cattle as a poisoned batch of feed, stating it would be investigated; and since no one had seen Greta's body, her death was announced later from a heart condition, blaming the excitement of the festivities. It all calmed things a little, but still a few dozen protestors stood at the palace gates and they didn't only blame us. Some placards blamed Dawn Mandrake and her sons, saying they had brought the darkness back with them and demanding they be banished once more.

Isaac was here, called from his marriage bed; along

with my sister, the Mandrakes, and our uncle. Isaac and Thomas were debating a plan of action.

"This entity appears ruthless and powerful and we need to find the same energy in which to deal with it. We will work on this all day and come back to you this evening with a plan. We must enact some spell as soon as possible to stop this as I fear its power is growing stronger."

Everyone left except my sister, who urged me back into bed to rest. "You can take the tincture, I'll get Ramona to make you some." She said stroking my hair. I nodded and let her arrange it, but the moment she left me to rest, I dismissed Ramona, and gathered my grimoire and a couple of other spell books and began reading voraciously. I left the drink on the table. After a couple of hours study, I asked my guard to escort me to the Mandrakes' property. I wanted to check on Dawn to see if she was doing okay and ask her advice with some ideas I had about incantations. If she thought they could be of use, I'd go find Isaac and Thomas, but I didn't want to interrupt them if it just seemed like the whimsy of a largely untrained witch.

My powers were raw, but they were strong. It swirled around me like electrical currents, and it needed an outlet. I'd been practising for a while now, but it wasn't enough. Truth was, I wasn't sure of what exactly I was capable of. I'd been too scared to try. What if I went out of control; a ticking time bomb?

Dawn let me in after my guards had checked the house again. Stationed outside, I walked down the long corridor behind Dawn as she led me into the kitchen.

"Have you settled in, Dawn? It's rather a bit larger than your last accommodations isn't it?"

"It is and at least there are no protestors right outside my windows. It's lovely and secure. No one around to bother me at all."

"Except two sons." I laughed.

"Yeah, that's true." She replied, going to fill up a pan with hot water.

Then she turned back around to me and my blood ran cold.

Dawn's eyes were black, her head tilted toward me, and her smile was evil.

"Honey, I'm home." She said, and she laughed maniacally.

CHAPTER ELEVEN

Leatha

I was frozen in place, but my mind remembered the words from my dream.

'Your return to the past will give me my future'.

I thought it had been the planes, and an entity from there which had traveled back with me, but it was Dawn who I'd brought back with me.

My mind just couldn't equate the wonderful woman I'd known with what stood before me.

I had to use some magick and fast.

"I call-"

"Continue that sentence and I shall kill this body." The entity spoke.

"Dawn, please."

"My name is not Dawn Mandrake. She is but a vessel for me. One that seems to be proving strong enough to carry my soul."

"So who are you?" I asked.

The body moved slowly and jaggedly, like a computer glitch. "I'm a wronged sister. Years ago, I should have ruled Andlusan. The first rules remember? But they found me wanting, delicate, and gave the throne to my sister instead. And when I studied the dark arts in order to gain the strength to get my crown back, my sister banished me to the planes. Trapped me between realms. Years I've been there, imprisoned, watching, waiting, gaining strength from the dark souls cast there. And then you came and I recognised your blood, my family. And so because of you I was able to return. Meld myself to your DNA because we share genetics."

"Who are you?" I asked it again.

"My name is Tatiana. I'm your grandmother's elder sister." Walking toward me she lifted a hand and trailed an icy finger down my cheek. "And I've returned to take what's mine. Andlusan."

I watched as her eyes began to bleed.

"Nooooooo. This body cannot fail me. I need it. I will be back for you, Leatha." She screamed, her mouth forming a garish horrifying grimace.

And then Dawn dropped to the floor, blood dripping from her mouth.

I ran as fast as my shaking legs would carry me, adrenaline forcing me to move, as I called for the guard and Lord Thomas. Then I went back and felt for Dawn's pulse. It was barely perceptible, and I screamed a tortured scream.

Dawn was fighting for her life and yet her husband was unable to be at her side. Instead he was working with Isaac to find something to heal her before it was too late.

I sat with my sister in her chambers.

"There has to be something we can do." Mercy paced her room.

"Do we know anyone who can speak to the dead? Not the necromancer, but someone who can converse with those who have passed on to the next world?"

"What you refer to is called mediumship. I've not heard of anyone here in Andlusan who can do that. We would need to ask Isaac."

I shook my head. "I'm not asking anyone else. It would put their life in danger. This is on me. I'm going to look up how to contact those who have passed on and then I'm going to the mausoleum to speak to Grandmother."

Mercy's body tensed up. "Leatha, you can't! It's too dangerous. You don't know enough."

"And you didn't know anything about travelling the planes, but you did it. To save me. To save Billy. So now I will take a chance to save Andlusan."

At that, my sister's shoulders slumped in defeat. "Then I will read along with you. We will do this together. Just as we rule."

I nodded because for studying it would make things easier, but when the time came to challenge Tatiana, I had no intention of my sister being part of it.

The next day Dawn remained unconscious, although she was showing small signs of improvement. I set off for the mausoleum, hoping that I had learned enough to contact my grandmother, though I doubted my abilities. Mercy had insisted that Lord Thomas sit at his wife's bedside and had requested that Isaac gather together every witch and warlock he knew and bring them to the palace grounds.

Opening the door, I took the familiar walk to the tomb containing my grandmother and stood before it.

"Hey, Grandmother. I don't know if you get to watch over us, but if you do, I'm sure you must know what is happening right now in Andlusan. Tatiana is here. My carelessness caused it. I am so very sorry.

Everything you taught me, and I brought a malevolent spirit that is already causing death, destruction, and chaos. The village is at war. I need you, Grandmother."

I placed a candle in the middle of a black plate at the foot of the tomb, lit it, and recited the spell I'd been learning.

"Blessed Goddess who holds the key
 Pray listen to what I ask of thee.
 For Grandmother Raine will you open the door
 And let her spirit return to the place where she lived before."

An icy breeze passed through the tunnel and a haziness shimmered in front of me. Then there she was, exactly as I remembered her from my childhood. My Grandmother Raine.

"Child, I cannot stay long, and you must not summon me again. Those who have passed should be left in peace. As you have learned, when you meddle with spirits and travel uneducated you can cause untold damage."

I dropped to my knees; head bowed.

"I'm sorry, Grandmother."

"We have no time for apologies. We have to capture Tatiana before it is too late."

I looked up at her. "Tatiana has yet to find a host strong enough. How do we capture her? What did you do before?"

My grandmother's image flickered in and out. "Tatiana wanted to rule, but she was prone to madness. We were close as sisters, as close as you and Mercy; but when they announced I would be queen, it broke Tatiana further. She asked if we could rule together and I said no. It was the biggest mistake of my life. She swore revenge and now she is back." Grandmother's eyes widened. "She has realised who is strong enough to host her."

"Who?"

"Her own kin."

I leaped to my feet. "Mercy? She has Mercy? Grandmother, what do I do?" I wept as I spoke. I couldn't lose my sister. Not now. Not when we'd just grown so much closer.

"Look at me and listen to me, child." My grandmother said.

So I did.

CHAPTER TWELVE

Leatha

As I returned towards the palace, all hell had broken loose.

"What's going on?" I asked one of the guards.

"The villagers who were protesting heard of the witches and wizards of the village being gathered together to be brought to the palace. They met them at the village square and they are holding them prisoner until you and Mercy come speak with them. We've sent guards, but at the moment there is a standoff as they have weapons and are threatening to remove the old ways."

I shivered.

"Okay, I will make my way down there. Please

assemble a team to accompany me, and I request my sister joins me immediately. Where is she?"

"She has been visiting Lady Mandrake. I shall send someone to collect her and meet you at the square."

I nodded and began my journey.

Crowds jeered as they saw me.

"Witch. You bring blight to our land." One shouted. Others jeered similar things and some spit at the ground as I walked by. My guards cleared the way for me to climb onto the stage. There was no sign of Mercy and I realised that I had this moment now; me, alone, to talk to my village and ask their forgiveness for what I had done.

It took some time, but the guards brought the crowds under control and they were silent while I spoke.

"I have a tale to tell you and it is not a pretty one. It's a tale of selfishness, but I am hoping it will also be a tale of redemption, of lessons learned. If you hear me speak, afterwards I will arrange a vote and if you no longer accept me as Queen, I will abdicate my position."

Murmurs started amongst the crowds but the guards closed them down.

I took a deep breath. "Before my reign I thought I

learned magick, and I travelled the planes to a place called Earth."

There were gasps amongst the crowd.

"But I did not learn my craft properly, crudely attempting magick and risking my life, all in the name of trying to have fun. And all because I found my life in Andlusan, my future life of being responsible for all of you, so very wearisome. It was only a short time ago and yet that spoiled and inconsiderate child is no longer. Instead, before you is a woman who has realised that the craft that runs through her family's veins, is something that like anything of worth, should not be used without guidance and teaching. When our mother stopped the use of white magick, she inadvertently drove it underground.

"I became trapped while travelling and had to be rescued. But it appears I brought back a spirit. The spirit of a great aunt. This aunt wishes to rule Andlusan and is trying to possess someone strong enough so that she can take revenge on our village. She wishes to rule and I fear her rule involves each and every one of you doing her bidding. Her spirit is on the loose and it is my fault.

"The only way we can battle her is by all joining together to fight with pure white magick. I understand that some of you have no belief in the old ways and think it is all a route to the demons of the world, and I ask; no, I beg; that you have faith in me, even though I don't deserve it. I, your Queen.

"When the unruly spirit is contained, I will ban all travel from Andlusan through magick, to keep us all safe. I will arrange teachings about the old ways for everyone, whether you wish to practice it or not; and I will ask that those of you who have no faith in the craft, also study in ways to keep those who do accountable. We shall form a proper court to include all and you shall vote to decide if my sister rules alone."

I looked out over the crowds, watching Mercy weave her way through and ascend the stage to the side of me.

The crowd remained silent, waiting for her to speak.

Moving towards her, I clutched her arm.

"Mercy, we must act fast, before it's too late. Tatiana is coming for one of us. We are strong enough to hold her."

Mercy's head tilted to the side.

"That's right. One of us is." A sinister laugh echoed around the square and she shook my arm off and addressed the crowds.

"My Kingdom. I am Tatiana, your new Queen, and those who do not pledge allegiance to me shall die." She touched the guard at the side of her and his veins began to become visible black streaks up his skin and he screamed in pain as his skin blackened and burned.

"Now." I shouted, and I made my own soul float out of my body and let my grandmother in.

I watched, hovering, as my grandmother in my body addressed the panicking crowds. The witches amongst them began to chant the spell that Isaac had been teaching them.

"Goddess, Mother, one so strong
 Bind our will so we are one
 Wrap it around she who doesn't belong
 And with our will let the evil be gone."

They chanted it over and over, but Tatiana just laughed. "You're not strong enough. There are enough here who do not want the old ways. Come join me." She shouted at the crowds. "I shall need an army. We shall take over all the kingdoms."

A man ran to the stage and climbed on.

"I am with you, my new Queen. Let your power have us rule all the land."

She brought him to his feet, but as she did, the black veins travelled up his arms and his hand blackened. His eyes went wide, and he pulled his arm away screaming.

My body looked out over the crowds and my grandmother's voice rang out. "My strength is fading. This is your last opportunity before Tatiana rules us all. Say the spell, I beg of you, and I will give my soul to save you all."

My body dashed over to that of Mercy's, and the battle of our grandmother and Tatiana began.

"Ana. Listen to me. You don't have to do this. You were right. We should have ruled together. I was wrong and for that I apologise, but this is not the way. These bodies will not hold us for long. Even strong within your own kin, soon you will begin to weaken. Do you wish to kill your own family? Your great niece?" She held out a hand. "Come with me, Ana. I will come to the planes with you. Let us rule there. In the darkness, in the quiet, in the place of lost souls, let us rule together to try to free those stuck in the void. Sisters ruling together, as it should be."

Mercy/Tatiana looked out over the crowds who were now all still and staring at the stage. By now, almost all were chanting the spell.

Then Mercy's body started to travel with the black veins and she held a hand in front of herself.

"If you kill your own kin, you are as mad and as unfit to rule as they always said you were." My own mouth uttered with my grandmother's voice.

Tatiana grabbed my grandmother's hand and shouted "together," and just like that they were gone and I jolted back into my body and grabbed my sister who cried out in pain.

Isaac dashed to the stage, followed by a number of other witches. They began healing chants, and I watched in amazement as the black veins disappeared and my sister opened her eyes.

"What in the Goddess' name just happened?" She asked before fainting.

CHAPTER THIRTEEN

Leatha

If I said what followed next was a happy ever after, I would have been lying. The month that followed was one of protest and discourse. But this time those who opposed the old ways had a voice and were represented on the council.

Eventually, it was decreed that only those who had studied white magick with a qualified witch or wizard would be allowed to use it, and that protection of Andlusan would be joint between those who practised and those who didn't. Two separate armies with one common intention. To keep Andlusan safe. It would never be perfect, but then nothing ever truly was.

Dawn recovered, though she would always have a

weakness in her lungs that gave her a permanent cough and a shortness of breath that limited her movement. But she was just glad to be alive and be with her reunited family.

On the day of the voting—the day that the village would decide whether Mercy ruled alone, or we ruled together—we once again took to the stage in the village square. Mercy spoke of how the two of us combined had defeated Tatiana, and how although I had made mistakes, I had learned major lessons from them.

When I addressed the crowds, I said simply that I would rule for the people and no longer saw myself as the focus. That if they allowed me to continue to rule, it was my plan to travel to the different courts alongside the emissaries and help maintain peace in all the kingdoms. Mercy would stay in Andlusan.

When the results of the vote were counted, they had chosen to keep me as joint ruler. I stood on that stage and vowed to never let them down, to fight for them with my last breath.

And someone shouted up from the crowd that they'd already seen me demonstrate that when I had given up my own soul to fight for theirs.

Ten years later

"My goodness me, you have grown so tall, Prince Henry." I hugged the thin, gangly, dark-haired boy who had rushed over to meet us.

"Henry always beats me." A dark-haired tomboy of a girl with hair that looked like it needed a good brush ran up panting. "Auntie Thea, it's not fair."

I leaned over to her. "He won't beat you to the crown though, will he? First rules, right?" I winked.

My niece, Gwendolyn, looked thoughtful, sticking her tongue in her cheek. "Unless I decide to rule jointly with him, so that I can travel like you do. Though my friends say it's 'girls rule and boys drool'."

"Well, there's plenty of time for you to decide, given that you are only eight years old, and I don't think your mother and I are planning on going anywhere any time soon." I rubbed the top of her head as my sister approached.

Mercy stepped forward and hugged me. "Long time no see, Sister."

"Indeed. I see you have been busy again in my absence." I pointed to her once more rounding belly. "Is five children not enough?"

She smiled. "No, though I think this shall be the last one."

Aaron walked over and with the way he still looked at his wife-nine years after marrying her in a joint ceremony with Billy and I-I wasn't sure Mercy was right.

"Brother." Aaron hugged Billy, clapping him on the back. "Come, let's grab a drink and let the women chatter."

"Still a pig, I see?" I shouted after him.

Aaron just laughed.

"Go on then." I said to my own husband. "You may as well rest now, because in a week we're expected at the Spring Court."

He didn't know yet that I was lying, and that we would be staying in Andlusan for some time with our family, while I prepared for the birth of our firstborn. We had been trying for a long, long while and I couldn't believe it was finally happening for us.

"You wear me out, wife." Billy grumbled good-naturedly.

"As does mine, but I'm not sure we are talking about the same thing." Aaron quipped.

I guffawed with laughter. Things had changed for us all on return to Andlusan, but some things were exactly the same. Family and our love for each other. The most important things in the world.

ANNOUNCEMENT

To Queen Leatha and Prince William
A girl, Princess Raine Tiana; and a boy, Prince Thomas Aaron Isaac.
The family are all doing well.

THE END

IMMORTAL BITE

Enjoyed Royal Rebellion?

Try another paranormal romance by Andie M. Long

IMMORTAL BITE

He vowed to never love again, but now his undead heart is beating…

She finds it hard to keep living; is he her salvation?

Since his turning, Caleb lives in his remote country estate with a skeleton staff. His beloved rose garden occupies his time; a tribute to his past lost love, along with a sharp reminder that the thorns that would scratch a human leave no lasting mark on a vampire.

Artist Vivienne dreams of a garden and a stranger, feeling compelled to sketch roses over and over. When the name Tetburn Manor whispers on the edge of waking, she finds the house and gardens that match her dreams and sets off to sketch them, wondering if the house can lift her constant melancholia.

Caleb watches Vivienne as she herself blooms while she paints his garden standing outside of his estate. Should he listen to his heart and let her in?

Warning: this book mentions self-harm.

ABOUT THE AUTHOR

Andie M. Long is author of the popular Supernatural Dating Agency series amongst many others.

She lives in Sheffield with her son and long-suffering partner.

When not being partner, mother, writer, or book editor, she can usually be found on Facebook or walking her whippet, Bella.

FOLLOW ANDIE

Andie's Reader Hangout:

www.facebook.com/ groups/1462270007406687

(not a street team, just a place to hang and have fun).

Mailing List:
(get a free ebook of DATING SUCKS on sign-up)
www.subscribepage.com/f8v2u5

ALSO BY ANDIE M. LONG

PARANORMAL ROMANTIC COMEDY

SUPERNATURAL DATING AGENCY

The Vampire wants a Wife

A Devil of a Date

Hate, Date, or Mate

Here for the Seer

Didn't Sea it Coming

Phwoar and Peace

CUPID INC

Crazy, Stupid, Lazy, Cupid

Cupid and Psych

PARANORMAL REVERSE HAREM

FILTHY R$CH

Filthy R$ch Vampire Playboys

Filthy R$ch Vampire Husbands

NEW ADULT PARANORMAL ROMANCE

SISTERS OF ANDLUSAN

Last Rites

First Rules

PARANORMAL ROMANCE

Immortal Bite

CONTEMPORARY ROMANCE

THE ALPHA SERIES

The Alphabet Game

The Alphabet Wedding

The Calendar Game

The Baby Game

Box set of books 1-3 available

THE BALL GAMES SERIES

Balls

Snow Balls

New Balls Please

Balls Fore

Jingle Balls

Curve Balls

Birthing Balls

Upcoming: Balls Up

STANDALONE SUSPENSE TITLES

Underneath

Saviour

MInE

WOMEN'S FICTION

Journey to the Centre of Myself

<u>WRITING AS ANGEL DEVLIN</u>

Contemporary steamy romance.